MW01138691

A Beard Tangled in Dreams

The True Story of Rip Van Winkle

Steve Wiley

Ordering Information:

Quantity sales. Special discounts are available on quantity purchases by bookstores, corporations, associations, and others. For details, contact the publisher at the email address above.

Orders by U.S. trade bookstores and wholesalers may also order directly from Ingram Spark.

ISBN: 978-1-7353046-2-5

Also by Steve Wiley

The Fairytale Chicago of Francesca Finnegan

The Imagined Homecoming of Icarus Isakov

Part One

Falling Asleep

Untold Dreams

THE ORIGINAL *RIP VAN WINKLE* WAS A MEAGER SIXTY-four pages. Quite short for a tale spanning twenty years. Why so short? None of those pages accounted for all the years that languorous legend spent asleep. The story captures just two days: the day Rip fell asleep and the day he woke up. Apparently, his sleep was so deep, it was without even a single dream. There has never been a single published word of what Rip dreamt all those years, until now.

It's hardly surprising Rip's decades of dreaming have gone unpublished for so long. Of what importance is a lifetime of dreaming? To most, dreams are inconsequential, rarely-remembered nothings of the night. To most, dreams don't matter. To most...

It would be wise to take dreams seriously. After all, they sometimes change the course of human history. Einstein dreamt the theory of relativity. Sitting Bull dreamt his victory over General Custer. Harold Dickson dreamt the exact location of the richest oil strike in history. The father

of quantum mechanics dreamt the structure of the atom —
nucleus, electrons, and all. Larry Page dreamt Google.

There is a price to be paid for not taking dreams
seriously. Abraham Lincoln prophetically dreamed his own
assassination. So did John Lennon. Journalist William
Stead dreamed the Titanic sunk, and without enough
lifeboats. He boarded the liner in defiance of the dream and
was last seen clinging to a raft with John Jacob Astor shortly
after the infamous sinking.

Countless dreams are conveniently forgotten or
brushed aside. What of all those forgotten dreams,
consigned to oblivion? What divinations, inventions, and
miracles lived in those dreams? What stories?

Rip Van Winkle is one of those long-lost dream stories.
It is a tale so intricately woven with dreams, it could only be
fully explained from within that unexplainable midnight
realm. It is in that realm the story of Rip Van Winkle will
for the first time be truly told.

Not that the original story was a total lie.

Some of what the world knows of Rip Van Winkle is
true. More is untrue. Most is untold.

First, what was always true: Rip was an extraordinary
figure who lived in the rather ordinary village of Catskills, a
Dutch hamlet in what was then the province of New York,
a British colony. The village was named after the Catskill
Mountains, which loomed with legends over the townsfolk
and were the source of many a mystical tale. Rip was well-
liked by all in town, with the exception of his wife, Dame
Van Winkle. Rip's laid-back lifestyle and inability to
provide even the most basic of necessities were faults she
could not forgive. Rip was a master of idleness who would
rather "starve on a penny than work for a pound," as author
Washington Irving originally wrote. He idled around the

countryside fishing, napping, playing, doing anything but earning a living. One night, he idled himself to the extreme, falling asleep for a remarkable twenty straight years.

As for the untrue, the Catskill Mountains were not haunted with the supernatural. There were no mysterious, nine-pin-playing ghosts rolling balls with a sound like thunder that echoed through the mountainside. No one tricked Rip into drinking an enchanted, sleep-inducing liquor. He needed no help drinking liquor and passed out fairly often on his own. And while it is true Rip slept the years away, the sleep was not dreamless. No, it was quite the opposite.

The dream is the untold. As is often the case, the untold story is also the most intriguing one. Everyone has untold stories, too outrageous or dangerous to be told — the secret romance, the promise broken, the battle lost. Rip's story is all of these things, and more. One doesn't sleep for two decades without experiencing everything from the wildest of dreams to the worst of nightmares.

In Which Rip Gets Drunk and Falls Asleep in the Wilderness

THE DAY OF RIP'S DISAPPEARANCE WAS AN ESPECIALLY unproductive one, even by his standards.

Having gone to bed early, Rip woke late. He hurriedly dressed and slipped out of his bedroom window to avoid the authoritarian Dame Van Winkle. There was much work to be done around the house and farm, but the day was far too pleasant for that. It was a summery sort of autumn day, one better suited for fishing. Rip grabbed his twig of a fishing pole and set off with his dog Wolf toward the Hudson River and the sanctuary of those still vast, unexplored woods.

That forest was a frontier one, much different from the forests we know today. Frontier forests were enclosures. Once inside, there was little proof of outside. The only evidence of anything other than the forest was the occasional patch of sun or moonlight, but those appeared less and less the deeper one wandered through the trees. The trees themselves were thick and crowded, the paths narrow and overgrown with roots and reeds. Many a pioneer was swallowed by those woods, never to be heard from again.

Not Rip. Having grown up in the forest, Rip navigated them as well as any wild, woodland creature. He whistled without a care as he zig-zagged through the trees, Wolf hopping along as the two descended toward the river valley. It wasn't long before they reached the hilly boundary of woods, where they stopped to look down on the colorful, fast-flowing river. The colors were from the leaves. Trees wept them into the river, flecking the foamy surface with picturesque tears. It was a fine river-fishing view.

Rip cared more about the view than the fish. He found himself a cozy nook in the roots of a shaggy willow with ample shade. He baited the dull, rusty shard of metal he used for a hook with a freshly dug earthworm and cast a line beyond the floating leaves.

Rip wouldn't catch anything that day. He never caught anything. That wasn't the point. The point was to relax, and relax he did. He lay back, the wind composing woodland lullabies with its shuffling of the leaves. Shadows danced heavily upon his tired eyelids. He propped his pole against the tree, closed his eyes, and was soon fast asleep.

Rip slept soundly, for there was not so much as a nibble on his line to wake him. He slept so soundly the whole day passed him by without his noticing. It was a bark from Wolf at a passing chipmunk that finally startled him awake. He was even more startled by the sight of the sun sinking behind the mountains. His wife would unleash hell should he return home without dinner. He reeled in his line, praying hopelessly for a fat fish to please her, but there was nothing.

Rip leapt up and rushed into the forest for other game. He had traps set throughout the area that needed checking, and quickly. He must make it home before nightfall. Luckily for Rip, he was a slightly better trapper than fisherman. It wasn't long before he came upon a mangy-looking squirrel he'd trapped. Better than nothing. He hurried home with it.

Dame Van Winkle was waiting for him. She was a perilous sight. His hateful other half stood still and sullen as a gargoyle sculpture on the front porch. There was a humorless look on her hatchet-face, her sinewy arms folded rigidly across her broad chest. Rip wondered how long she'd been waiting for him as he walked nervously up to the house. He would not be invited inside.

"Evening, wife." That was Rip's way of assessing her mood.

"I trust it was a gratifying day." That was her way of assessing his productivity.

"Aye. Caught a fine squirrel, plump as a partridge he is..."

Rip trembled with fear as he held up the not-at-all plump trophy by the tail. His wife stared angrily at the rodent for a few long seconds before stomping down from the porch. She slapped the squirrel from him with one hand and his face with the other. The swift and unexpected combination sent the henpecked husband to his knees.

"WHERE in the name of jumpin' Jehoshaphat have you been all day, Captain Queernabs?" she screamed.

It is unclear to this author who Jehoshaphat was, or why he was jumping. Captain Queernabs, on the other hand, was a humiliating vulgarity used in those days to refer to a shabby, ill-dressed fellow. It was also Dame Van Winkle's nickname for her browbeaten husband.

"Err... Fishing? No, sleeping... No, squirrel hunting!" Rip stammered as he rose to his feet.

"Well, while you were out hunting starved squirrels, you failed to repair the fence!" Wolf interrupted the castigation, snapping up the neglected squirrel for his own supper before darting away. "Because you failed to repair the fence, our only cow has escaped!"

Rip looked at the decrepit wooden fence surrounding his miniscule farm. It looked to have collapsed from a puff of autumn wind. Rip was miserable at the thought of repairing it. He hated farm work, because he hated the farm itself. It was an easy farm to hate. It sat on one of the most pestilent scraps of earth in all the New World. Weeds flourished in the garden, suffocating the few vegetables which somehow sprouted in the dry, nutrient-less soil. The chickens lay robin-sized eggs. Snakes ate the eggs. Weasels ate the chickens. The pigs ate each other, for lack of feed. This all left very little for the Van Winkles to eat. The cow was the only reliable provider on the cursed farm.

"That cow is the only reliable provider on this cursed farm!" Dame Van Winkle yelled. "That creature is worth more than you. Find it! And don't dare return here without it!"

She slammed the door with such force the doorknob flew off. It tumbled down the porch to Rip's feet, as if to say, "Don't come back."

He wouldn't.

INSTEAD OF LOOKING FOR THE COW, RIP LOOKED FOR A tavern. A tavern would be much easier to locate. Rip took the proverbial path of least resistance to his local watering hole — the King George Inn. The quaint, two-story red brick cottage sat on a grassy hill at the edge of town. It was an unassuming establishment, and could easily have been mistaken for an ordinary house, were it not for the faded plaque of the royal namesake swinging above the door.

Rip's heart rose at the sight of the candle-lit windows glowing like cheerful beacons against the fading night sky and mountains. He could see the inn was busy from the smoking, dancing, and drinking silhouettes in the windows. He hurried up the narrow, rocky path to the front door.

Dimly lit, mostly from a candle-wax-drenched chandelier and smaller oil lamps on each of the tables, the place was comfortably full of folk. They were idle personages mostly, but also a scattering of persecuted husbands. Rip was both, so the crowd welcomed him with a mighty cheer. Before he had the chance to bow his thanks, Nicholas Vedder, the landlord of the inn, handed him a powerful pumpkin porter. Rip raised his glass, and finally felt at home.

Rip was welcomed to a corner table by a friend and fellow farmer named Vance Van Dijk. More listener than talker, Vance always leant a sympathetic ear to Rip. He was secretly fascinated by Rip's seemingly endless misfortunes at home and abroad. Rip drank quickly, finishing his first porter before the conversation had even begun.

"What brings the venerated Van Winkle out this evening?" Vance asked, suspecting there was something wrong, because that was generally the case. Rip was also drinking faster than usual. Drinking speed strongly correlates to the seriousness of the reason for getting drunk.

"A cow," Rip muttered.

"How dare you slander her eminence, Dame Van Winkle," Vance joked. "Say rather bovinae-succubus, or plain ole' bitch."

"No, God's honest truth," Rip laughed. "I lost the cow."

"Shame, that is. I suppose you were sent here to look for the stray beast?"

"Aye."

Sorry to say, but I have not seen a cow in these parts. May I recommend a strategy for finding this wayfaring heifer of yours?"

"You may."

Vance signaled to Vedder for another round.

"From where we're sitting, we have an unobstructed view of the king's highway." It was true, they sat at the front window of the inn which held a view of the road. "The strategy is to remain here, imbibing until the cow passes by, at which point we shall spring out and recapture her!"

Rip of course agreed to the "strategy." He had no hopes of finding the cow that night. He hoped only to drink, and drink he did. Rip drank all his cares away and then some. It wasn't long until he was drunk as a fiddler's whore, poor as a church's mouse, and without a worry in the world.

Once Rip had rid himself of his last dollar, he leapt onto the table for a song to celebrate his latest conquest of capitalism. The inn quieted as he cleared his voice.

THERE'S MANY MEN GET STORE OF TREASURE
yet they live like very slaves:
In this world they have no pleasure
the more they have, the more they crave.
Hang such greedy-minded misers,
that will ne'r contented be.
I have heard by good advisers
that content lives merrily

. . .

Rip bowed to loud cheers from all in the inn. He stumbled off the table after the fourth or fifth bow, but was quickly helped up and nursed back to health by a fresh porter.

The alehouse jollity continued late into the night. Vance and Rip were the last two there. The last one at the bar has a reason for being the last one at the bar. Rip's reason was straightforward. He had nowhere else to go. Dame Van Winkle would not have him back without the cow. The wilderness was just as unwelcoming. If he could go anywhere, it would be to the past. To a girl.

"Have you seen Rosie about the village?" Rip asked Vance hopefully.

Rosie O'Ryan was the one Rip had meant to marry. Rosie grew up just one wheat field away, which was close as could be in those days. The two had been inseparable as children. They walked to school, skipped school, scaled mountainsides, rolled down valley hills, hunted for lost treasure, got lost hunting for lost treasure, caught fish, skimmed stones, dammed streams, and all the rest. They were the closest of friends.

Rosie grew up and into a beautiful woman, the object of all the town's affection. Rip grew up and into a druidic, colonial-era hippy, the object of no one's affection, or attention. Still, Rosie and Rip had been deeply in love and would have wed, if couples married for love in those days. Marriage back then was largely a matter of property and practicality. Rip had neither.

Still, Rosie would have married him had her father not promised her to a wealthy landholder of the gentry, twice her age. She had been married off against her will and shipped far away to a manor by the sea. Rip had not seen her in years, but she was often in his thoughts.

12

"I'm sorry to say Rip, but I've not seen your Rosie in forever," Vance answered. "Whispers around town say she had a baby boy not long ago. Big as a whale, they say. Don't reckon she'll be back in these parts anytime soon. She was just too fine a specimen for the Catskills. Too fine a specimen..."

The news, while not surprising to Rip, was heartbreaking. He had no children of his own. The thought of a child with Dame Van Winkle was utterly terrifying. A part of him had always held out hope Rosie would return, and they would be reunited. Rip looked out the window to the road, for some sign of Rosie. Instead, he saw the cow.

"The cow!" Rip shouted.

"The strategy has worked!" Vance triumphantly declared.

The roaming cow spotted his master in the window and waddled up the hill to the front door of the inn. Rip drank his last waking drink for years before staggering out the door and grabbing hold of the cow's collar. He used the collar more to keep himself from falling than to keep the cow from getting away. Nicholas Vedder followed his last guest out, giving him a table lantern to help light his way. Rip thanked him and started down the road toward home.

Rip needed the lantern. The night was not just black, it was wraithlike. The few village lamplights were blown out on account of the blustering winds. Rip stumbled drunkenly along, clutching the cow, doing his best not to fall to the ground as he swayed left and right. The cow led the way. Rip was lucky to keep up, for as long as he chose to.

The pair soon came to a fork in the road. Rip knew it. One way led home. The path home was wide and well-trodden. The other way led up into the mountainous wilderness. That path was narrow and less traveled.

The cow took the road home. Rip stood there, watching the animal trot slowly into the darkness as he considered his own road. It wasn't an easy choice. The road home was a predictably miserable, unwelcome one. The road into the mountains was a peculiar and perilous one, its ending unforeseeable.

Rip took the path less trodden, feeling free as the wind whistling through the woods. He whistled himself, relieved at having for the moment escaped the clutches of Dame Van Winkle. A world of possibilities, of self-rule and redemption, lay before him. He had no idea where he was going, but knew in his heart it was the right way. That hopeful heart led him higher and higher onto the mountainside, deeper and deeper into those untraveled woods.

Rip's newfound sense of hope would not last long. He was passing through a glade when a great gust breached the thin case of his lantern, leaving him totally in the dark. Had his dog Wolf not found him in that moment, his story may have ended then and there. The faithful dog led his master further into the wilderness. They traveled on and on, up and down, here and there, to who knows how, why, or where.

Chance brought them to a wide meadow, brimming with daisies. Rip recognized the place, even in the dark. He'd played there as a boy. He stopped and stared at the place, illusions of the past playing upon his dimmed senses. Apparitions of children played at hide-and-seek. Some rolled and wrestled through the flowers. Others blew the bulbs off dandelions. The wind sounded like their laughter. The moon shone bright as a boyhood sun for a fleeting moment. It was then Rip saw her. There was Rosie, golden hair shining through the night like stardust as she raced across the meadow. And there was a young Rip, chasing after her into the shadows of the trees.

A bark from Wolf returned Rip to the present. Time to move on.

The daisies bowed in the wind like a host of tiny white knights honoring Rip as he set forth on his legendary, unlooked-for adventure. Rip pissed in the face of one of the knights as he looked up to the night sky. Lightning flashed on the horizon. Thunder grumbled. Wolf sniffed that familiar scent of rain, growing stronger by the second. A storm was about to join them.

The two ran across the meadow. The rain waited until they were under the trees on the opposite side, so that they were mostly sheltered from it, at least for a while. Rip jogged after Wolf down a hardly noticeable trail, which wound around trees and bushes, but kept on steadily up the mountain, and into the thickest of woods.

Lightning flashed more frequently the further they traveled, helping to navigate the slim path, and exposing the gnarled, gnomish faces of the primeval trees. The trees stared amazedly as Rip passed them by because they were amazed. Humans had never before journeyed in those parts.

A deafening clap of thunder echoed through the woods. The cloudburst breached the protective canopy of leaves above. Rip was thoroughly soaked in just seconds. He stumbled through the dense woods after Wolf, the two desperately seeking shelter. All seemed hopeless, until Rip saw the dog disappear as if by magic into the base of a sprawling tree. Upon closer examination, Rip found it to be an immense, hollowed out oak.

Rip leapt inside, where he collapsed into a dripping, drained heap. The frequent lightning flashes illuminated his woodsy chamber. Not a single drop of rain fell from the vaulted ceiling, too tall and dark to guess the height. The fungus-covered ground was soft, warm, and dry. Wolf lay next to him, watching the chaos unfold outside.

Rip closed his tired eyes, a teardrop joining the raindrops on his face. He was ashamed at his present state. He was scared for his future, or lack thereof. He was nostalgic for a past that was gone forever. Wolf licked away the rain and tears, and with them the worries.

Comfortably sheltered from the storm, it wasn't long before Rip fell into his long, infamous sleep. Before he slipped away, he thought of Rosie. He wondered where she slept that night. He pictured her in the tall tower of some secluded castle sleeping comfortably in a feathered bed with silk sheets and goose pillow. He wondered if she might be thinking of him in that moment.

He wondered if she might be dreaming of him.

Part Two

Where We Dream

The Last Lighthouse Keeper

EVERY LIGHTHOUSE DIFFERS IN APPEARANCE, BUT ONLY one differs in purpose. It sits within the Sea of Dreams, a stone's throw away from Wakefulness, but not so far from Oblivion as one might guess. It stands closer to Yesterday than Tomorrow, because there is always more of Yesterday than Tomorrow in dreams. Far more.

All have seen its beacon, illuminating those flickers of consciousness in the remnants of night, casting a light on all those puzzling visions and events, impossible to fully understand or recall. The beacon itself is a navigational aid, though not in the normal, nautical sense. The ordinary lighthouse beacon serves as a navigational aid for ships at sea. This lighthouse serves not maritime pilots, but dreamtime ones. Its function is to protect, guide, and in some cases rescue all those lost dreamers. The beacon marks hazards of the dream seas, subconscious shoals, nightmarish tidal surges, and more. The lighthouse offers safe harbor in the dead of night.

The principal lighthouse keeper was a dream. Not that he was dreamed by anyone in particular. Or that he was much of a dreamer himself. He was one of those who resides in dreams, like so many other sentient beings happened upon in the deepest of sleep, most mistaken for concoctions of the psyche, or imagination.

Being a dream, the lighthouse keeper was nameless. You see, dream-folk are not ordinary people, bound by the cycle of birth and death. They are the symbols and manifestations of the collective unconscious. They are the wise old man before he was Gandalf the Grey. They are The Hero with a Thousand Faces. They are every villain that same hero overcame. They are the everlasting ideas we transform into all those mythologies which give sense to the world.

That said, it would not do to tell this tale without a name for this particular dream. He is far too important a character to remain a nameless archetype. We will call him Deacon, because that is an authentic name, and this lighthouse keeper was authentic as you would guess any lighthouse keeper to be. Deacon also happens to rhyme with that foremost instrument of his occupation — beacon.

Deacon wasn't the last lighthouse keeper back in those days, but he is now. Sadly, most lighthouses have since been unromantically automated. He wasn't always the *principal* lighthouse keeper. He started as assistant lighthouse keeper. Lighthouses generally had at least two keepers, sometimes three. Deacon was promoted to principal lighthouse keeper when the former principal keeper went mad, proclaiming himself an albatross before throwing himself from the top of the lighthouse. More than a few dreamers lost their way that night.

Most lighthouse keepers are mad. It tends to help with the job. The seclusion, irregular hours, and monotony of the routine don't attract commoners. Deacon was uncommon, but not unhinged. He was sane as most, though he didn't look like most.

Deacon was a faun, but only in appearance. Fauns are known for their love of spirits, sex, and skullduggery. They worshipped Dionysus, god of grape-harvest. The cult of Dionysus and its secret, orgiastic rituals have always been strongly associated with fauns and centaurs.

Deacon was different. He preferred water to wine. He was more sober than sexual. He looked more ordinary man than mythology. He looked like a lighthouse keeper. Two stubby horns pointed through his bucket hat. Baggy trousers covered his hairy goat legs. Wide eyes emphasized the wrinkles on his face. It was hard to say his age because time is not measured where we dream.

Time is a geographical feature of dreams, as opposed to an irreversible sequence of events. A voyage to Yesterday or Tomorrow simply requires charting an accurate course. Echoes of waking time do sometimes pass through dreams. They do so as a distinct wind. The four classical compass winds have been well established, but the fifth has not. The fifth is that of ordinary time passing in dreams. It is unmistakable from other winds in that it has a color to it. Good times blow a swift blonde hue. Lifetimes pass steadily from green to gold. Anytime is a hardly noticeable, powder blue zephyr. Each time has its own marked shade.

When Deacon wasn't watching the sea, he was content perceiving the many-colored winds. Between the sea and sky, the faun was quite immovable, and rightly so. He was a lighthouse keeper, and even in dreams that is a stationary profession. Deacon wouldn't have had it any other way. His world was the faraway lighthouse and the speck of sea stone it sat upon.

The lighthouse itself was one of those towering, tree-shaped ones, thickest at the bottom, narrowing on the way to the top, where it was crowned with a shiny, brass cupola. The body of the tower appeared ivory-colored from a distance but was in actuality partially translucent. Looking closely, one could see a service room here, a gallery there, perhaps a faun hurrying up the spiral staircase, or reading within the lantern room. The translucent effect was a result of scattered light fragments from the beacon atop the lighthouse. That beacon was lit by no ordinary flame. The light from it illuminated everything from the darkest depths of the subconscious to the highest heights of dream castle ramparts. Its range and penetration were immeasurable.

Deacon passed his working hours in the lighthouse and his resting hours in the quaint stone cottage extending from the base of the structure. The cottage was the keeper's quarters, within which was every amenity to make one feel comfortably at home. There was a bed, bath, parlor, pantry, and all the necessities required by someone living alone on the island. Deacon had even built for himself a pleasant private library, complete with wood stove, smoking chair, and a vast collection of literature. A voracious reader, Deacon spent much of his time in the library.

A day (or night) in the life of a lighthouse keeper was one of solitude and tranquility, but also of labor. Labor came first. Deacon started his day at dusk, the crash of waves breaking on the beachrock acting as his alarm clock. His first duty was to the light. Polish it. Fuel it. Spark it. Before his nightly watch set in, there was more work to be done. Something always needed an oiling or a painting. Deacon passed lifetimes oiling and painting. Then there was breakfast (or dinner) followed by tea. A lighthouse keeper *always* has a strong black tea on hand —sustenance for the long and lonely watch.

The watch was a meditative ritual, well suited for a faun of Deacon's naturally reserved disposition. He looked inward, even as he looked outward. Time sailed by with the wind, as did the occasional dreamer. After the watch came a nap, followed by another meal, then a book. He was most at ease in the library, accompanied by words and the warmth of a fire.

It was there he first noticed something was wrong.

HAVING JUST FINISHED HIS WATCH, DEACON SAT BACK in his smoking chair, hooves upon the ottoman, billiard pipe burning slow as the stove fire, book in hand. He read *Peter Pan* that night. *Pan* wouldn't be released for over one hundred years, but that didn't matter. Deacon had sourced the title from a rare bookseller based in the far reaches of Tomorrow. Of course, our all-seeing lighthouse keeper had observed Peter, Hook, Tinkerbell, Tiger Lily, and the rest from afar, so he enjoyed the story immensely. Neverland was not a far voyage from the lighthouse. '*Second star to the right, straight on till morning,*' was just a tad closer to morning than the lighthouse. He sometimes saw Peter soaring through the strange stars, deeply dreaming children in tow.

Deacon was startled from the story by the creeping suspicion that something was wrong. He first noticed a peculiarity in the wood stove, where the flames danced ever-so-slowly back and forth, like a pendulum. As it turned out, the fire was dancing *with* the lighthouse, which was swaying from the fast-growing winds outside.

The lighthouse keeper hurried to a porthole window, where he beheld the strangest of storms. The rains came not from above, but from below, and the drops themselves were not water, but wildflowers. Blossoms of every color assailed the lighthouse like flocks of butterflies. The air was so thick with them, Deacon couldn't see six feet in any direction.

Deacon was surprised, which in itself was surprising. He was used to sudden, unexpected changes in the weather. There is no predictable rhythm to the climate in the Land of Nod. Seasons may change overnight, and in no obvious sequence. Winter may follow spring, or summer for that matter. The sun sometimes sets instead of rising. The moon sometimes outshines the sun. The stars may shine from the sea, instead of the sky.

In severe weather, Deacon's duty was to the light. He put out the stove fire and put on his wellies, raincoat, and mariner's cap. Hurrying out of the library and into the lighthouse, he started up the spiral staircase leading up and along the walls of the tower, winding round and round, like some never-ending nautilus shell.

There was no railing, so he kept as near to the damp, stony walls as possible. After spiraling up only a few stories, he started to feel queasy, and not so much from the walking in circles, but from the wind. It continued to shake the lighthouse with a force Deacon was unaccustomed to. He worried the whole lighthouse might topple over into the sea.

Deacon's cap flew away the moment he popped his head out and into the storm from the hatch leading to the topmost platform. The floral scent was overpowering. He felt drenched with perfume as he emerged, carefully shuffling forward to the railing. The beacon still shone glaringly, giving him a better view of the unusual conditions.

Peering out across the sea, the faun could hardly believe his eyes. Wildflowers burst from the water in great spouts, swirling into the sky in a chaos of every color. Those flying flowers were a strange sight, stranger than any tempest the lighthouse keeper had yet braved, and he'd braved countless. Stranger still was the surface of the water, which appeared gone altogether, having been so thoroughly dusted in flowers. Still the waves rose and fell, making the sea look like a series of ever-shifting, paint-splattered hills.

It wasn't long before the flowers blinded Deacon, covering his eyes, filling his mouth, clogging his nose. Momentarily disoriented, a gale nearly sent him soaring over the edge and into the raging waves below. He clutched the railing with one hand, wiping the flowers from his face with the other. He retreated back down the hatch into the shelter of the lighthouse to collect his thoughts, feeling quite defeated for the time being.

"This is all wrong," Deacon muttered to himself as he plucked impaled carnations from his horns.

The storm was too curious and catastrophic to be coincidental. The winds were blowing wildly toward Wakefulness, the currents flowing swiftly in that same direction. That in itself was unusual. Normally, the winds blew the opposite direction, carrying dreamers to that deep, difficult to recall mystery of Oblivion. By blowing toward Wakefulness, it was as though the forces of nature were trying to oust some foreign invader, like a sick person expelling an infection. Deacon had seen these conditions before, but never so severe. They were generally caused by a lost, or lucid dreamer, overstaying their welcome. Lost dreamers are a danger to dreams and themselves.

Deacon warmed himself with cup of tea as he looked out his kitchen window for some sign of the storm's end. There was none in sight, but there was a rare, nine-tailed fox. It sat perched on top of a group of great boulders near the shore. Nine-tailed foxes are animals of ill-omen, often appearing deep within storms or other disasters.

Deacon finished his tea and ventured outside. He ducked through the rain-flowers toward where the fox sat. The fox saw him and slipped through a hardly noticeable crevice in the rocks. Deacon squeezed through the same crevice. It led to a grotto, where lived the only other resident of the island — a mermaid.

She was no ordinary mermaid. That particular mermaid traveled far and wide, swimming the endless and bottomless Sea of Dreams. She was always the first to know of wayward dreamers, and everything else. She was one of those rare precognitive dreams that warns of some great catastrophe, or salvation.

The stillness of the cave was a welcome change from the storm outside. The shallow waters were calm, glowing violet from the coral below. Deacon walked to the end of a rocky ridge leading to the center of the pool, looking for some sign of the fox or mermaid. The fox was nowhere to be seen, but it wasn't long before the mermaid rose to the surface.

Being a dream, the mermaid was a nameless fantasy from the dawn of maritime legend. She wore a pearl circlet woven with her wavy, pumpkin-orange hair. Her skin was an ivory to match the lighthouse. The jade and silver of her tail glittered like jeweled seaweed in the coral-light. Her lips were amethyst. Her sapphire eyes twinkled at Deacon. They always twinkled at Deacon. He never seemed to notice.

"Some storm out there," the faun declared.

"Why must you insist on commencing every conversation with the weather?" she teased. "Is it intentional? Or are you accidentally the most boring conversationalist on our island?"

"Intentional. I am a lighthouse keeper. Weather is my business. Also, profound topics are better addressed after trifling ones."

"Ah, but in this case, you know very well this weather *is* profound. Maybe you should have paid me a compliment before starting the conversation on such a profound note?"

There was an overtly seductive tone to her voice. She was always seducing the lighthouse keeper, or attempting to. The attempts were generally lost on the daft Deacon.

"What do you make of this storm?" Deacon asked. "It is unnatural to be raining wildflowers from the sea."

"You are unnatural! There floats before you the consummate seafaring fantasy, the original goddess of nautical folklore, the romance of every sailor's sea shanty. Yet, you hardly notice," she splashed him notice with her tail. "You would rather tend your precious beacon, read your lifeless books, and question me about the weather than join me here in my private bath."

She wasn't wrong, and Deacon knew it. He blushed, steering the conversation back outside.

"I believe this tempest to be a matter of grave concern. Just now, I saw a nine-tailed fox scurry down here. Such a sign bodes ill. I have not seen a nine-tailed fox since before the flood. Come, tell me what you know of the storm. Have you heard the cause of it?"

"Of course I have heard the cause of it. If I tell you, what will you tell me?"

"What do I have to tell anyone?"

"Secrets. Poems. Secret poems. All lighthouse keepers are poets. I see you through that little porthole in your ivory tower, head down, scribbling sonnets, lost in some secret world. How will it go? *In a Wonderland they lie. Dreaming as the days go by. Dreaming as the summers die..."*

"Ever drifting down the stream. Lingering in the golden gleam. Life, what is it but a dream?" Deacon finished for her, while also acknowledging her claim to be true. Deacon was indeed a poet. Most lighthouse keepers are, though not the sort to share them with the world.

"If not a poem, a secret would suit me," the mermaid continued. "A secret worthy of telling, that is."

Not only do lighthouse keepers keep secrets, they fish for them. Most waking fisherman also fish for secrets, though few realize it. The typical fisherman casts his line of hope into the wild blue yonder, hopeful the forces of fate will answer his call. Fish for long enough and all those secrets of the universe can be caught: the meaning of life, the nature of reality, to be or not to be. Fish for long enough, and the depths will disclose their own dreams.

"What will it be? Poem, or a secret?" the mermaid asked.

"Neither!" Deacon negotiated. "Your terms are extortionary..."

"Then you may as well return to your lonely library of luminosity. Better yet, climb to your post and observe the never-ending storm. Watch the untold numbers of dreamers blown to kingdom come. Watch them sink to the bottom of the sea. Watch the lost dreamers stay lost..."

Returning to the lighthouse empty-handed was not an option. The scope of Deacon's lighthouse-keeping responsibilities extended beyond the beacon in that particular scenario. It was his duty to ascertain the cause of the storm, and if possible, settle it. Should he stand idly by, the storm might further strengthen, eventually consuming the lighthouse and his beacon, casting an infinite darkness over the Sea of Dreams.

"One secret," Deacon offered.

"The secret must be worthy of revealing," she countered.

Deacon begrudgingly agreed, shaking her clammy hand.

"Now, the storm. Tell me of the source."

"Whispers from Oblivion speak of a cause — an errant dreamer, of course. They say he has been dreaming for weeks, months even."

"I'll have to find him. What is this errant dreamer's name?"

"Rip Van Winkle."

"I'll have to remember that."

"If the rumors from Tomorrow are true, it's a name you won't soon forget."

There is a mountain lifting sheer above London, part crystal and part myst. Thither the dreamers go when the sound of the traffic has fallen. At first they scarcely dream because of the roar of it, but before midnight it stops, and turns, and ebbs with all its wrecks. Then the dreamers arise and scale the shimmering mountain, and at its summit find the galleons of dream. Thence some sail East, some West, some into the Past and some into the Future, for the galleons sail over the years as well as over the spaces, but mostly they head for the Past and the olden harbours, for thither the sighs of men are mostly turned, and the dream-ships go before them, as the merchantmen before the continual trade-winds go down the African coast. I see the galleons even now raise anchor after anchor; the stars flash by them; they slip out of the night; their prows go gleaming into the twilight of memory, and night soon lies far off, a black cloud hanging low, and faintly spangled with stars, like the harbour and shore of some low-lying land seen afar with its harbour lights.

~ Lord Dunsany, A Dreamers Tales, 1910

The Sleeping Siren

DEACON DIDN'T IMMEDIATELY SET FORTH IN SEARCH OF Rip. He waited, hoping by some miracle the storm would settle on its own. But the weather only worsened. Immense plumes of smoke veiled the moon and stars, further darkening the night. Thunder joined the regular roar of the sea. Rain mixed with the flowers, turning their petals to sopping globs of mud. The lighthouse was stained with every color known to man. It rose from the sea like the stray end of a rainbow.

Deacon reluctantly decided to leave the comfort and safety of his island home. His first destination would be the Sleeping Siren Saloon, where he hoped to hear some news of Rip Van Winkle. A haven for deviant dreamers, the Siren was not your typical public house. It was named after those beguiling fiends who lured sailors with enchanted voices to shipwreck on their stony shores. The Siren attracted night-time sailors with a different sort of song. Instead of drinks, the bar served secrets, wishes, memories, and all of those other unseen desires from the waking world. Deacon occasionally visited for a drink or two. He drank a common, friendly spirit, which helped to fend off the lighthouse loneliness.

Deacon set forth in the only boat he had — a rickety dory, until then used only for fishing. Luckily, the Siren was a short journey. On clear nights atop his lighthouse, Deacon could hear its echoes of laughter and see its lights glittering merrily over the far horizon. Not that night. The storm above had settled somewhat, but lived on in the sea below. The waters were rough as ever.

Deacon was no skilled sailor. A lifetime of lighthouse duty left him quite unprepared for any prolonged rowing excursion. The moment he cast off, he looked (and felt) like a sorry speck of half-goat debris tossed about at the whim of the never-ending sea. It took every ounce of energy he had to keep the piteous boat upright, and even more to propel it forward. As he struggled along, he looked back at his lighthouse, already wishing he had never left. It wouldn't be the last time he wished for that.

Our reader may be wondering why, being a dream, Deacon did not simply fly to his destination. It is true, some have been known to fly in dreams. It is also true that those laws of nature which govern our waking world do not in all cases apply to the world of our dreams. But there are still laws shared by both realities. Grass is green. Water is wet. Happiness is transient. So is sadness, and most everything else. Lions devour zebras. Intellectuals devour books. And principal lighthouse keepers simply cannot fly.

The flightless faun rowed painstakingly along. By the time he finally reached the tropical atoll where the saloon stood upon a high sand dune, his boat was half-filled with rose water. He huffed and puffed as he heaved the wooden tub toward shore. He moored the boat to a flimsy dock, wondering why as he did so. The boat looked ready to sink at any moment, and the dock ready to break apart. Boat tethered, he plodded up the steep sand dune where a beacon of a different sort shone down on him — tavern lights.

Taverns come in all shapes and sizes. Most are made for the customary revelry, filled with friendly faces and the scent of hops and barley. Some taverns are silent and sad, meant not for those who want to drink, but who *have* to drink. Others are barren, filled only with echoes of the past and roaming ghosts of patrons hazily reflected in the dusty etched mirrors. The Sleeping Siren was an unpredictable combination of all these, often changing with the whim of the night.

Inside, Deacon found the place freshly painted with the dazzling brush of candlelight burning in dozens of straight arrows toward the sky. The candles were everywhere: shining within bottles, standing on tables, hovering in mid-air. The candlelight created marvelous, ever-changing shades of garnet and gold. It seemed to Deacon the saloon was without a single shadow, and what was more, it was without a ceiling. The candles reached up and into the stormy sky. By some protective spell, the halo of candlelight sheltered the tavern from the elements.

The Siren was comfortably full of dreamers. There were lucid dreamers, deep dreamers, and in-betweeners. Lucid dreamers were in a fully conscious state, sipping secret cocktails and mingling with other like-minded patrons. Deep dreamers were zombie-like, staggering about the place like overserved barflies, saying little, remembering less. In-betweeners were those in a half-conscious state, most sitting at the bar looking confused, others dancing awkwardly about.

Deacon stepped up to the bar, which glowed faintly

from the candlelight dancing in the mirror behind it. He was joined by Benjamin the bartender, a highly sought-after sage of spirits. Benjamin was a friend to Deacon, and everyone else. He was asleep and dreaming in his home as he tended the midnight bar. Benjamin was an oneironaut, or an especially skilled lucid dreamer who explores dream worlds for a living. He looked the part. Wiry arms and legs were hidden under a steampunk-ish waistcoat and breeches. Long, curly locks of copper flowed from under his stovepipe hat. Sleeping eyes shone bright in the candlelight.

"One-hundred-thousand welcomes to our not-so-solitary-lighthouse-keeping-defender-of-darkness!" Benjamin greeted. "Join me for a glass of cheer. You look like you need it!"

"A glass of free will is more like it, Benjamin. I'm feeling more fatalistic than usual."

"Free will is an illusion. Lucky for you, illusions are our specialty." Benjamin got to mixing the drink as he chatted. "What brings you out on such a treacherous night? Talk around the tavern says this storm has no end."

"It will have no end, unless we find the beginning. It is the storm that brings me here. There is a rogue dreamer by the name of Rip Van Winkle, who has been asleep for untold nights."

Benjamin served up the autonomous concoction. It looked strong and tasted stronger. After just the first sip Deacon felt a tingle of spontaneity course through his veins.

"Sleeping for that long you say?" Benjamin questioned with a hint of skepticism as he lit his long-stemmed pipe from a nearby candelabrum. "Such a yarn is the fabric of fairy stories. I have heard it told Sleeping Beauty slept for one hundred years. King Arthur supposedly sleeps away the centuries under Camelot..."

"The fabric of this realm is woven with fairy stories," Deacon explained. "Every mythology, legend, and creed originates in dreams. That is why the same mythologies get retold all over the world — they occur here first, where they are beheld by the slumbering masses of mankind. It is no coincidence the same great flood-myth has been retold everywhere from Mesopotamia to Mesoamerica. That deluge happened here, when the sea first swelled with secrets. *Snow White* is another sprawling weed of a motif. In Europe, it's *Snow White*. In Africa, it's *The Girl with the Star on her Forehead*. *Sleeping Beauty* is no different. As it turns out, she was a French princess in a fever dream, who steered herself wildly off course. She ended up a castaway on a secluded sandbar. Rescued her by chance as I was passing the island on shore-leave."

"Well, I'll be jiggered. No prince awakening her with an enchanted kiss then?"

"No. A kiss would, and did, make for a better ending. That princess had no interest whatsoever in waking up. I sailed with her kicking and screaming toward morning. If a prince happened to be there when she woke up, he'd have been more likely to receive a cuff than kiss."

They were interrupted by a clumsy old man who stumbled into a nearby patron. A ludicrous bar fight ensued. Neither combatant was accustomed to punching in a dream. The two thrashed about with odd muscle twitches and the occasional slap. The candles circled slowly about the pair like spectators, careful not to be knocked over and put out for the night.

"Tell me Benjamin, have you seen any sign of this Rip Van Winkle? There may not be much to distinguish him in appearance. I hear he is a yeoman from the colonies."

"We've had plenty of colonials about, all drunk as lords

on liberty and latitude. It is a deceitfully powerful concoction. Sends em' reeling every time. Those two stampcrabs had their fill just before you came in," Benjamin pointed to a pair of pantless men in bobbed wigs, cackling like mad. "From Philadelphia, I think. Colonial dreams are strong as ever these days. Won't be long until the whole of that territory tries some in the night, then wakes to rebellion."

The bartender puffed his pipe in thought, sending smoke rings of all shape and shade soaring throughout the saloon. The rings whirled playfully around dreaming patrons, occasionally colliding with a puff into someone's face. No one seemed to mind. Why would they? Surprisingly few smell anything at all when they dream.

"Come to think of it," Benjamin continued, "there was a curious colonial in here some time back. If I remember rightly, he was not drinking the usual fare. This fella imbibed nothing but memories, and not just any memories. I'm talking an unhealthy amount of distilled remembrances, real as you and me. Left here so pissed on nostalgia he could hardly stand. Me and some of the regulars helped him out and on his way. He set adrift toward Oblivion, a condition he was already fully in."

"Did he say anything at all?" Deacon asked. "What was the cut of his jib?"

"He talked to himself. Mostly crying into his memories, watching visions of yore twirling in the firelight. He may have asked for the whereabouts of someone, though I can't recall who."

The bartender put down his pipe and poured himself a drink.

"He was dressed like a common colonial, but it was plain to see his heart was uncommon. One can only truly know a fella meeting him in dreams. With the polish of civilization stripped away, you see the man for what he really is. You see the secrets, frailties, the passions. I saw in that man a soul so utterly possessed with the past he was without a present. There are dreamers like your princess who accidentally find themselves lost, and then there are those who were meant to be lost. I say that man was one meant to be lost, and never found again."

"When was this?" Deacon asked, suspecting the peculiar patron to be none other than Rip Van Winkle.

"Hard to say. I remember it was a fair evening. Come to think of it, the storm set in not long after."

"You say he set a course toward Oblivion? If he was so possessed with the past, why would he not sail for Yesterday?"

"If he'd had any control over his bodily functions, he might have done just that. He was hardly able to sleepwalk himself out of the saloon. We helped him into a dinghy. When he wakes up, if he wakes up, his recollection of this place will be an unsolvable puzzle of pictures."

Deacon drank the last of his free-will, dregs and all. The drink was working its magic, but he had a taste for something stronger. He was feeling unimpeded, but also nervous.

"I planned more for a jaunt than an expedition. Suppose I have no choice but to set sail in search of this character. A glass of adventure may have suited me better than the free-will."

"My shift is up soon. You're off to Oblivion, and I'm headed in the opposite direction. Shall we drown two birds with one stone? One glass of adventure for the last call, and a glass of morning for me."

Benjamin served up the adventurous concoction. It was

a sparkling, ruby-colored tonic in a tulip glass, two maraschino cherries with a buccaneer toothpick-sword through them. The bartender poured himself a highball glass of what looked like liquid sunrise.

"Fare thee well." The two clanked glasses.

The moment the bartender put the charmed tonic to his lips, he began to fade away, slowly disappearing in time with the drink. When the drink was all gone, so was he, dissolved into a mist which rose and disappeared into the storm.

Benjamin the bartender had of course woken up. Deacon wished he hadn't. He sat nursing his adventure, hoping for more to drink, and more advice. If only there were more like the bartender — more lucid dreamers, there would be less lost ones. Oblivion was filled with the misguided. The voyage there was a perilous one. The region was vast and uncharted. There was no telling who or what Deacon might find. There was a chance he might find nothing, or worse, that he might lose himself.

Luckily, the glass of adventure went straight to his head, then over it, to the tip of each horn. A wanderlust seized his whole being. The thought of returning to the lighthouse was gone from his mind. He fantasized of riding rolling waves, slaying sea monsters, rescuing shipwrecked sailors, of finding and waking this delinquent dreamer, Rip Van Winkle.

Deacon swigged the last of his adventure, and set forth on his own.

On the following night [dreaming], I wandered to the northern land and found myself under a gray sky in misty-hazy cool-moist air. I strive to these lowlands where the weak currents, flashing in broad mirrors, stream toward the sea, where all haste of flowing becomes more and more dampened, and where all power and all striving unites with the immeasurable extent of the sea.

Someone is standing there. He is wearing a black wrinkled coat; he stands motionless and looks into the distance. I go up to him — he is gaunt and with a deeply serious look in his eyes. I say to him, "Let me stand beside you for a while, dark one. I recognized you from afar. There is only one who stands this way, so solitary and at the last corner of the world."

He answered, "Stranger, you may well stand by me, if it is not too cold for you. As you can see, I am cold and my heart has never beaten."

"I know, you are ice and the end; you are the cold silence of the stones; and you are the highest snow on the mountains and the most extreme frost of outer space."

"What leads you here to me, you living matter? The living are never guests here. Well, they all flow past here sadly in dense crowds, all those above in the land of the clear day who have taken their departure, never to return again. But the living never come here. What do you seek here?"

"My strange and unexpected path led me here as I happily followed the way of the living stream. And thus I found you. I gather this is your rightful place?"

"Yes, here it leads into the undifferentiable, where none is equal or unequal, but all are one with one another. Do you see what approaches there?"

"I see something like a dark wall of clouds, swimming toward us on the tide."

"Look more closely; what do you recognize?"

"I see densely pressed multitudes of men, old men, women, and children. Between them I see horses, oxen, and smaller animals, a cloud of insects swarms around the multitude, a forest swims near, innumerable faded flowers, and utterly dead summer. They are already near; how stiff and cool they all look, their feet do not move, no noise sounds from their closed ranks. They are clasping themselves rigidly with their hands and arms; they are gazing beyond and pay us no heed — they are all flowing past in an enormous stream. Dark one, this vision is awful."

~ *A dream of Carl Jung, founder of analytical psychology, 1914*

Strange Seas

Returning to shore, Deacon discovered his boat sunken in the shallow harbor. The only sign of it was the stern, which peaked from underneath the waves like a crocodile beak. An alluring, white-sailed sloop had impudently docked directly above where Deacon's boat rested on the sea floor. The sailboat was his only option, and a good one. Feeling quite free from the free-will still coursing through his goatish veins, he commandeered the vessel.

The way to Oblivion is well known to all, even you. Oblivion is where all that mysterious absence of consciousness goes in the middle of the night. It is the realm of that deep sleep which goes unremembered, with all those countless, forgotten phantasms. In the case of dreams, unremembered should not be confused with uneventful. Oblivion is a boundless jubilee of knavish, night-loving spirits.

Deacon rarely passed through Oblivion. When he did, he was careful not to venture very far into it. Oblivion was not just vast, it was never-ending. Its incomprehensible size

41

was attributed to the fact that nearly all dreams are, in fact forgotten. Much of that territory remained not only unexplored, but unfathomed. Stories told of mythological monsters too ghastly for reality, hordes of exorcised demons, unholy avatars from the dawn of civilization, and the like. In other words, there is often good reason for the dreamer to forget the place. Many a midnight sailor with seafaring skills far surpassing Deacon's took that journey, never to return.

Deacon looked back again toward Wakefulness and the lighthouse as he cast off. He saw his beacon through the haze of steadily falling flowers, and the pale curtain of morning beyond it. The beacon burned bright as ever. It wouldn't need tending for some time, nor would it be worth tending if the storm didn't clear. Still, he would much rather be sailing that way.

The stolen sails caught a fine, flaxen breeze that sent Deacon speedily along. The sails were a welcome change from the ponderous oars he had been rowing. He stood smiling at the ship's helm, steering through the rough seas. The sailboat hardly needed his help. It rode the waves with ease, gliding up and down with such smoothness, the faun wondered if he weren't riding a fish.

Deacon sailed on, wondering why he didn't sail more often. The wind caressing his goat-fur, the seesawing sensation of the sea, and the freedom from his many mundane responsibilities felt more magnificent than he'd imagined possible. Having made a living observing sailboats from on high, he was ashamed at not having owned one of his own. He promised himself then and there that he would build a sailboat when he returned, and sail it at every opportunity.

Deacon soon came upon the outskirts of a wide

whirlpool, reminding him the sailor's life was far from perfect. Whirlpools were not uncommon in the Sea of Dreams. In the waking world, whirlpools are caused by opposing currents. In the slumbering one, they're caused by opposing ideas; the push-and-pull of the subconscious reservoir of urges and desires with the conscious sense of societal values and morals, as one example. Latent thoughts and demons living in the repressed depths of dream seas can be quite dangerous. Once in a while, these monsters rise to the surface, disrupting or devouring the unlucky sailor. Deacon had seen countless vessels sucked under the waves of a whirlpool, never to rise again.

Deacon thought he saw the pale scales of a leviathan peeking out from under the foam near the center of the whirlpool, so took a wide berth around it. Too wide, as it would turn out. Leaving the suckhole safely behind, he sailed on and on, and then on some more. He kept his eyes on the dim horizon, waiting for the shores of Oblivion to come into view, but they never did. With no sign of land, Deacon wondered if he had veered off course.

Sailing further along, the sea and sky began to change. The storm weakened. The hills of waves shrunk to hardly noticeable humps. The winds lost all color and fell to a whisper. The air became heavy and difficult to breathe. The water itself seemed thicker and discolored, even soupy in places. Deacon was most disturbed by his compass. The needle on it had disappeared entirely, as though there were no such thing as direction. The sailboat floated ever-so-slowly on, an increasingly lost lighthouse keeper at the helm.

Then he saw something in the distance. It was a fog bank of such immensity, it looked like a grey kingdom spontaneously risen from the sea. Its menacing walls of mist looked solid as stone. The kingdom was one of desolation, where no ships sailed.

Deacon did his best to steer away from the fog bank, but it was no use. An unusual wind possessed the boat. The wind was unusual because instead of pushing, it pulled. It came from a gate that had suddenly formed within the fog bank. Deacon sailed soberly through it, the effects of his glass of adventure worn off by what now looked to be a case of misadventure.

The density of a sea fog is not consistent. It may be filled with cavities, caves, and clearings of fresh air. That particular fog was crisscrossed with long tunnels like lanes intended for travel. Deacon was able to steer his ship down one of these lanes. It was a weird and winding way, dark as night in some places, light as a cloud-covered day in others. It went on for quite some time before Deacon saw anything but the sea below and gloom all around.

When he finally did see something, it was not the land he expected, but light. At first, it was no more than a flicker in the distance. He sailed toward the flicker, then saw another, and another after that. The lights were pale wisps of gold, blinking here and there under the water like submerged fireflies.

Deacon sailed on until he was surrounded by the eerie lights which seemed to multiply, and shine brighter, the further he traveled. He hadn't noticed it, but the further he sailed toward the lights, the darker the fog became. Eventually, it turned so pitch black, and the glow of the sea so bright, it was as though the water were reflecting the stars. Only, there were no stars.

Deacon bent over the side of the boat, staring into the sea to discover the source of the lights. Gazing deep into the murky waters, he thought he saw his own reflection, and was astonished at the sight of it. You see, the Sea of Dreams does not reflect, because it does not remember. Deacon had never seen himself in the water. He leaned down to get a closer look.

He soon realized the face he was staring at did not belong to him. It was the face of a princess. She danced for Deacon, whirling and twirling slowly under the surface. Her blood red hair swirled like seaweed around her glowing golden crown. Her mantle opened wide in the water, leaving little to the imagination. Her eyes seized his with such a stare, Deacon found he could not look away, try as he might. He leaned over the side of the boat until his horns were touching the water. Her face grew large as she swam up to the surface toward him.

She was face to face with him when in an instant her features changed. The skin on her face withered away, down to the very bone. Her hair transformed into a nest of octopi. Her eyes exploded into orbs of flame. Fish scales replaced the alluring mantle, her body below a rotting skeleton. The princess smiled ghoulishly with her undead face.

Before Deacon could move, bony hands like manacles of cold steel were upon him. They heaved his whole petrified body out of the boat and into the sea. Strangely, Deacon's sight was not blurred under the water. He opened his eyes to terrifying visions, clear as day. Corpses in varying degrees of decomposition paraded all around him, staring curiously at him as they passed. Some of their faces were shameful and sad, others proud and fair. Most looked serene as they marched to depths unseen. All were dead.

Deacon had strayed well off course, into the dominion of the dead. Dreams of the dead are more than mere projections of the dearly departed. They are the departed. Countless, verifiable stories throughout history recount deceased visitors relaying firsthand, impossible-to-know information to the living in dreams. The dying often dream of the dead because their paths have finally converged. As we age, the outside world fades, steadily losing its color, light, and love. As it does so, the world of dreams calls us more urgently, and we eventually heed that call. Not that Deacon was dying. He was just lost.

Dreams can drown like anyone else, and Deacon was about to. He had accepted his fate, and was preparing to join in stride with the rest of the dead on their march to wherever it is the dead go, when he felt another bony arm clench him by the collar. It pulled him up to the surface, hoisting his bedraggled body back onto the deck of the sailboat.

Deacon brushed the sopping fur from his eyes. His rescuer looked more damnation than salvation. The man was a tall, slender, and frightful figure. The cloak he wore matched the grey of the fog so perfectly, he looked partially invisible. His face was hardly noticeable in the shadows beneath his shaggy hood. He looked like the Ghost of Christmas Future, and that may have been possible, if they were anywhere near the future. The future was a different direction entirely.

"You, sir, are not the least bit dead," the man declared, his voice sounding ancient as the sea he was standing upon.

"I am in wholehearted agreement with that observation, and it seems I have you, kind sir, to thank for it," Deacon said as he scrambled up to his hooves, extending his soggy, trembling hand. "I am the principal lighthouse keeper. Thank you for saving me. May I ask who you are, and where I am, exactly?"

"I go by many names: Charon, Anubis, Tarakeshwara. I

am the Ferryman," he pointed into the water, where the dead marched on. "I escort souls of the departed across this river of dreams that divides the world of the living from that of the dead."

"Is that so?" Deacon pretended to be nonchalant, having not had the slightest idea he was on a river, let alone one brimming with souls. He had drifted further off course than he thought.

"I have one additional..." Deacon attempted, before being cut off by a wagon train which had burst forth from the sea, dangerously near the boat. The ghost train galloped swiftly by, riding the waves as if they were an established trail. The skeletal passengers gave a banshee wail, the echoes of which could be heard long after it had disappeared.

"I have one additional favor to ask of you, Ferryman," Deacon continued. "As you may have already guessed, I am in dire need of navigational counsel. I had originally set a course toward Oblivion, though must have been blown off course along the way."

"There is an estuary not far off." The Ferryman pointed a long, skeletal finger down an adjacent lane in the fog. "Not long after the lights disappear from the depths, a current will carry you windward. When the hue of the water changes, you will see the tips of trees on the far horizon. Those trees mark the entrance to that forest without end."

"Thank you, and my sincere apologies, but another question has just occurred to me. May I ask if you have come across one Rip Van Winkle? Dutch-American. Mischievous fellow. Overserved on memories. Seems he has been dreaming for some time, causing quite the disturbance.

I wonder if his story has already ended here, with so many others?"

"I did once ferry a Pappy Van Winkle. That was some time ago. The gentleman was overserved not on memories, but whiskey. He was the sort to drink this whole river dry."

"Perhaps a relation... Again, my sincere apologies for the trouble."

"No trouble. I have saved more than a few lost souls..."

Deacon watched as the psychopomp turned away, walking on water back to his ferry. The ferry itself was small and flat, like a skiff. The ferryman stood tall on it, using a long pole to propel the boat forward from the river bottom. He drifted away, the glow of the dead trailing behind him. He disappeared before he was far enough away to do so.

Deacon steered his sailboat cautiously toward the estuary. He stared straight ahead, careful not to look again into the haunted waters, or to come anywhere near them. He was by then beyond sober, and seriously reconsidering the sense of his one-man search party for this Rip Van Winkle.

He had just dried off when the storm returned, and a bite of winter to go with it. Bitter flower stems pricked him with cold. He longed for the warmth and comfort of his lighthouse. What he wouldn't give to rest his hooves by the fire, pipe smoldering with his stove. He would have a fine view of the storm, instead of a place within it. A good book. A strong cup of coffee, or tea. He wondered if they served such drinks in Oblivion. Surely they must. There was everything in that vast wildwood of imagination.

He wondered if there was also a Rip Van Winkle.

A dream! My sister, listen to my dream: Rushes are torn out for me; rushes keep growing for me. A single growing reed shakes its head for me. A twin reed, one is removed from me. Tall trees in the forest are uprooted by themselves for me. Water is poured over my pure hearth. The bottom of my pure churn drops away. My pure drinking cup is torn down from the peg where it hung. My shepherd's crook has disappeared from me. An eagle seizes a lamb from the sheepfold. A falcon catches a sparrow on the reed fence. My goats drag their lapis lazuli beards in the dust for me. My male sheep scratch the earth with thick legs for me. The churn lies on its side, no milk is poured. The cup lies on its side; Dumuzi lives no more. The sheepfold is given to the winds.

~ First ever written account of a dream, King Dumuzi of Sumeria, 3rd millennium BC

Every Enchanted Forest

DEACON WOULD SOON ARRIVE AT THE SAME PRIMEVAL forest visited by the Bronze Age king in his dreams so long ago. The first sign of it was not the trees, but the sea — its silver swells transformed to golden hills. Deacon hardly noticed at first. He sailed on, the barley fields below not so different from the water. Hills of grain rose and fell like great waves. Stalks swayed in the wind like whitecaps. Gusts blowing low through the fields made a ruffle like tides. Deacon saw little red farmhouses peeking out of the fields here and there like scattered boats.

He had not sailed far through the fields when he saw the first tips of trees described by the Ferryman peaking over the horizon. Soon, more treetops emerged on either side, all rising to dizzying heights. It wasn't long before his whole field of vision was filled with that ages-old forest of incomprehensible acreage.

That forest was the original enchanted forest, its seeds sprouting all those that came after: Sherwood, Mirkwood, Puzzlewood, and all the rest. The Beast lived deep within it, a rose-cursed recluse within his secret castle. Oberon and

50

Titania wandered through it upon a midsummer night. Peter Pettigrew escaped from it. Hansel and Gretel were nearly consumed by it. All have visited it in the dead of night, though few recall it.

The woods wailed a warning as the faun traveled toward them across the fields. Or were the woods traveling toward him? Whatever the case, Deacon wisely kept to his boat, entering the forest through a hardly noticeable gap in the trees where a narrow river flowed.

The forest was dense. Try as he might, Deacon could not see the sky through the treetops. The only evidence of it was the occasional stray flower from the storm which trickled through the canopy of leaves, but those were rare. The forest choir of swaying branches and rustling leaves was so overwhelming that at times Deacon found it hard to hear even his own thoughts.

The sailboat cruised down the twisting and turning waterway, thatched cottages with candle-lit windows passing by on each side between tall rushes. On the water, horse-like kelpie galloped, splashing past the sailboat into the heart of the forest. In the water, Deacon saw the faces of river creatures scowling and sniggering at him as they whizzed by toward the open sea. The river often rose. When it did, the faun felt as though the sailboat might take flight, soaring up into the air, straight through the treetops.

Deacon had not traveled far into the woods before he came across the first of many dreamers. Being Oblivion, they looked oblivious. Most wandered witlessly among the trees like lost children. Many were partially dressed or naked, reflecting either a lost sense of security or newfound freedom. Some danced with the trees. Some of the trees danced back. Others made love. Deacon stared in awe at reunions of star-crossed lovers, unfaithful husbands and wives, uninhibited orgies, and every other debauchery imaginable.

The woods were such an entrancing sight, Deacon fell into a trance himself, right there in the middle of the river, perched at the helm of his sailboat. He sailed blindly on, the lapse of time between his arrival on the river and his peculiar passage down it impossible to surmise. If one could recount time as it passes in a dream, it would be possible to ascertain how long he stood there, stupefied. It was likely quite long before the shadows interrupted him.

The shadows were hardly noticeable at first, because they blended in so perfectly with those of the trees. But when Deacon's eyes adjusted to the dim woodland colors, he saw them. They were everywhere. Some were small, fast-moving shadows, which ran playfully with his boat along the riverbank. Others were immense, like the shadows of giants bounding between the trees. Some shadows lurked in the river itself, swimming along the riverbed.

Deacon knew what the shadows were, having heard rumors of them from his faraway island home. The shadows were not dreamers themselves, but the *unrealized side* of dreamers, that unconscious aspect of the personality which the waking person is unaware of. The shadow's appearance and demeanor contrasted with that of their counterpart's waking experience. Because most tend to reject or remain ignorant of the worst aspects of their personality, the shadow is commonly evil. It is often linked to all those primitive, animalistic instincts superseded during childhood by the conscious, civilized mind. Everyone casts a shadow, which explains why there are so many.

The current slowed to a crawl. The shadows became more aware of the faun. They emerged from the trees to watch the curious creature as he drifted by. One particular shadow brought forth a tall, cheval mirror to the riverside. Deacon stared into the looking glass as he passed by, unable to see anything at first. The reflection was empty and motionless.

Then, there came a barely noticeable stir from deep within the mirror. Deacon saw a phantom standing within it, its back turned so that it faced the woods. As Deacon watched it, the thing lifted its head and turned slowly around to face the river, as if it was aware of someone watching. It stared at Deacon for a few long, unmoving seconds, head tilting with interest. Deacon stared back in the same way.

The phantom emerged from the mirror before Deacon could safely pass it. The figure was a shade darker than the other shadows. Gleaming eyes of emerald were all the light it shed. They drifted ominously through the forest like will-o'-wisps. When it approached the river, the other shadows cleared a path for it, as if by command. When it stepped into the river, it darkened the waters and stopped the current completely. Deacon's sailboat, and heart, stopped along with it.

The phantom grew taller as it waded through the waters so that by the time it reached the boat, it was tall as the trees. A wiry claw reached down from the treetops toward the terror-stricken lighthouse keeper. He leapt off the boat and into the river, frantically swimming to the opposite shore, where he dashed into the labyrinth of trees. Zigzagging through the woods, he heard the phantom howl as it splashed out of the river, rushing after him.

Deacon ran as fast as his cloven hooves would carry him, but the phantom was faster. He could hear it gaining on him, its bellowing breath piercing the forest. It was nearly upon him, when the woods sloped sharply downward, and he found himself out of his pursuer's line of sight for a few critical seconds. Deacon took full advantage, diving horns first into a dark, leaf-filled ditch. He lay there as still as could be, watching the phantom stomp by him at a ferocious speed.

It was many minutes before Deacon dared move a muscle. He lay there, convulsing from the cold and fear, teeth chattering, heart bulging within his fleecy chest. He wondered whatever he'd done to enrage the mirror-dwelling wraith. He wondered what the creature even was. It might have been a shadow, though it was much larger, darker, and more hostile than the others. Whatever it was, he seemed to have lost it.

Deacon rose from the ditch, a fresh wave of fear overwhelming him when he realized he was hopelessly lost. He set forth through the tangled forest to somewhere he could not recall. *Where* was he actually going? Was he looking for someone? Was it someone lost? He felt somehow different, and so did everything around him. Dreamers changed from roaming apparitions to still-life images. The trees were darker than nearer to the river, though he found he could hardly remember the river, or anything before it. Soon, he found he could hardly remember himself. He stroked his horns and pet his fur as if they were not his own.

The necromantic forest had cast its spell of forgetfulness on the faun. He wandered on, a stray dream who was himself deeply dreaming. He was oblivious to anything but the present, and spell or no spell, it was hard not to be. There, in the careless woods, scattered pillars of night flickered through chinks in the leaves, illuminating all that which is lost between our waking and dreaming lives. There were mythological creatures; bounding sphinx, upside-down mermaids with fish-heads and human legs, wolpertingers, werewolves, and more. A pygmy riding a feathered unicorn would have trampled Deacon to death had it not taken flight just before reaching him. Getting up was no easy task. Roots reaching to the nethermost pits of the human psyche emerged from the ground like tripwires. The trees and undergrowth were so thick and twisted, he didn't get on very fast, but that was fine. He was in no hurry. In dreams, the traveler does not rush to and reach some destination. The destination reaches him.

There were other lost dreamers. Rapturous children played hide-and-seek, crouching behind bushes and reeds before leaping out in surprise, chasing one another in circles around the trees. Romanesque sculptures roamed the woods like figures within some faded Renaissance painting come to life. Strangers embraced, many making love in beds of lichen and leaves. Most ran naked and free, as though it were the Garden of Eden, or an expulsion from the Garden.

Deacon had all of his clothes on, until someone took them off. He first saw her sitting upon a throne carved into the trunk of a bloated baobab tree. She did not look at all regal. She wore a faded white summer dress that hung loose and long on her, all the way down to her moccasins, which dangled playfully from the throne. On her head was a crown of common wildflowers. In the fickle forest light, her age was hard to say. One second she was a woman, the next a girl. Then a woman again. Whatever her age, she kissed with experience. She kissed Deacon as though it were his first kiss, and there is nothing so powerful as a first kiss, with the possible exception of a last kiss. After the kiss, she ran playfully away. Deacon followed her.

Within the river valleys of rest, there hide undiscovered kingdoms. Without knowing it, Deacon followed his lover straight into the ruins of one. Night magic was at work there, concealing the place within the greater forest all about it. Thick layers of ivy accosted the old buildings and flooded the once crowded streets so thoroughly, the ruins might have been invisible to someone standing just outside of them. As Deacon roamed the lanes, he heard furtive whispers from bygone days coming from abandoned homes. In the shadowy alleyways, he caught glimpses of ghoulish faces, glooming dark in the night.

Deacon and the girl wandered the empty streets, eventually making their way through a boggy courtyard and into a crumbling, reed-covered castle. He followed her through the reeds and over the collapsed castle gate. Inside, they walked down a wide, dark hall toward a dimly lit room at the far end of the castle. The sound of music and voices echoed from the room.

The room turned out to be a courtyard, with what appeared to be an eccentric royal ball taking place within it. Lines of torches blazed along the walls, casting light upon the revelers. The strange storm still raged above, and without treetops to obstruct it, soaked the guests in flowers. The guests themselves were an assemblage of all the odd creatures from the woods. Deacon was startled at the sight of a huge obelisk of a man with a lichen covered face beneath a thick red beard, long hair of autumn leaves, and two great horns sprouting from beneath them. A walking, talking cabinet strolled through the courtyard, brandy balloon in hand, cigar in mouth. Stained glass goblins joined hands in a circle around the living piece of furniture, tapping their boots together in a silly sort of square dance. A fine wind blew through the hall, hardly noticeable yet very much present, as if it were itself a guest.

On a throne at the far end of the courtyard sat the girl. A boy piper wearing a crown of red leaves played for her as he danced giddily about. Deacon made his way across the courtyard to the throne, where the girl leapt into his arms. The ball-goers made a circle around the two as they danced. Well, she danced. Deacon swayed. He was only a lighthouse keeper, after all.

She led the dazed faun around the courtyard as the guests cheered. She whispered songs to him as they whirled about. Deacon could make out individual words, but couldn't process whole verses. Imagine. Wish. Believe. *Forget.* The moment each word came out of her mouth it was instantly forgotten, carried away in the wind like sounds already in the distant past.

She kissed Deacon there in the center of the courtyard for all to see. This time it was a last kiss, and it sent him reeling. The moment it happened, the whole courtyard seemed to spin round and round with gravity-defying speed, as if he were riding an out-of-control merry-go-round. They spun and spun, going so fast, he and the girl eventually found themselves pinned firmly against the castle wall, paralyzed by the centrifugal force of the spinning courtyard. Deacon didn't mind. He didn't know who he was, where he came from, or where he was going. In that moment, he was no more than a feeling — the ecstasy of a carnival ride.

The spinning of the courtyard stopped as quickly as it started, causing the two to break apart with a startle. They were unexpectedly joined by a gale-force wind, which roared through the castle halls out of nowhere, instantly quenching every one of the torches lighting the ball. The confused crowd of muttering guests added to Deacon's own sense of confusion.

The wind fell silent and the entire ball was relit by the poof of a great bonfire that sprung up as if by magic in the center of the courtyard. Claps and whistles initially sounded from the crowd, as if it were all a planned segment of the night's entertainment. The guests then quieted, all eyes on the flames sending sparks into the night sky, where they set fire to the falling flowers.

The flames cast shadows on the crumbling castle walls. The shadows grew in size, before merging and taking the shape of that same phantom that had chased Deacon by the river. The monstrosity stepped from the castle wall into the ball. A path cleared for it as it made its way toward the bonfire. The crowd watched as the creature walked around, carefully scanning the courtyard for something, or someone. The faun trembled as its dreadful gaze passed over him.

The shadow began a slow dance around the fire, chanting low under its breath. As it danced, it spawned other shadows all around the courtyard, to the fascination of the ball-goers. The dark, approaching form of a sailboat circled the trim of the castle walls. Oohs and aahs sounded from the crowd. Deacon turned in amazement at the unlighted shape of a lighthouse upon a tapestry, its beacon spinning crazily. The shadows of a boy and girl could be seen chasing one another throughout the hall, up the stairs onto a balcony and down through the courtyard, meandering in and around the guests who gasped in wonder, then clapped in humor. The smoke from the fire formed the shape of a mermaid above the tips of the flames, rising higher in the air, where it swam about to claps and gasps from the crowd.

Then, several things happened at once.

First, the phantom found Deacon in the crowd. Its gleaming green eyes widened. It was as if the thing had just woken from a dream, or was a newly arrived guest in someone else's. The wind returned with renewed strength, whipping through the courtyard with a force that lifted the girl from where she sat on her throne, as easily as if she were a feather. She went spiraling up and into the flower-filled sky with a squeak of a scream that could hardly be heard above the howling wind. The last Deacon saw of the girl was her comet-like dot soaring through the storm.

Then, the bonfire was extinguished like a lone birthday candle, and the courtyard was cast into complete darkness. The phantom stopped his dancing, and for a moment, all that could be heard was the sound of the wind and drowned-out cries from the panic-stricken crowd. Cries of confusion turned to screams of terror when the phantom began devouring guests. It plucked them out of the crowd like appetizers, biting off limbs, and tossing partially eaten, dismembered guests aside. Strangely, the ball-goers did not die, or even bleed. Deacon watched in amazement as they ran limbless around the ball like half-butchered livestock.

The phantom stomped over the maimed guests toward Deacon, who retreated until his back was against the stone wall. Looking up, he could see the creature's hideously changing face clearly for the first time. One moment it was a skeleton, next a gorgon, then three gorgons, then the face of the faun himself. The thing stood over Deacon, laughing so deeply it sounded like it came from a dungeon below the castle. It convulsed as it laughed, growing larger and larger, eventually taking up half the courtyard. Deacon screamed for help but could hardly hear his own voice through the wind, still wailing a deafening blow. He raised his arms to motion for someone, but the air had become a blizzard of blowing flowers. They fell throughout the ball like celebratory confetti.

Just when it seemed all was lost, a light sprung up near the entrance to the courtyard. Deacon saw the silhouette of an elderly, cloaked man under a stray ray of starlight. The old man walked with the help of a staff toward the phantom, who turned to face him. The phantom stopped short of the old man, growing smaller as he faced him, yet darker.

The old man raised his staff. The phantom raised his claw.

The phantom struck at the old man, who blocked the blow with his staff before leaping forward and slashing his foe across the thigh. The phantom roared in agony, its blood a flowing, glowing emerald to match the color of its terror-stricken eyes. The blood stained the floor so thoroughly the courtyard began to look like an algae-filled pond. The phantom limped backward, fading into the castle wall from whence it came.

Deacon collapsed to the ground. He was relieved, but also exhausted from the ordeal, and his timeless wanderings in the woods. As he lay there, he noticed it had stopped raining flowers. He looked up at the ceiling. *How peculiar,* he thought, because all throughout the ball, there had been no ceiling. And the ceiling Deacon saw didn't look much different from no ceiling at all. The ceiling looked painted with glow-in-the-dark stars, as if the real stars had been frozen in time, a picture of exactly where they were in the sky that night. There were whole motionless galaxies above him as he lay there, half-conscious. The moon appeared, big and bright above him, laughing in his face. The moon was so bright, he couldn't see much of anything else, so he shut his eyes. When he opened them, the old man's face was where the moon's had been.

"Who are you?" the faun asked.

"I am the wizard."

I found myself passing through long vistas of trees which, as we advanced, continually changed in character. Thus we threaded avenues of English oaks and elms, the foliage of which gave way as we proceeded to that of warmer and moister climes, and we saw overhead the hanging masses of broad-leaved palms, and enormous trees whose names I do not know, spreading their fingered leaves over us like great green hands in a manner that frightened me. Here also I saw huge grasses which rose over my shoulders, and through which I had at times to beat my way as through a sea; and ferns of colossal proportions; with every possible variety and mode of tree-life and every conceivable shade of green, from the faintest and clearest yellow to the densest blue-green. One wood in particular I stopped to admire. It seemed as though every leaf of its trees were of gold, so intensely yellow was the tint of the foliage. We came to a darker part of our course, where the character of the trees changed and the air felt colder. I perceived that a shadow had fallen on the way; and looking upwards I found we were passing beneath a massive roof of dark indigo-colored pines, which here and there were positively black in their intensity and depth. Intermingled with them were firs, whose great, straight stems were covered with lichen and mosses of beautiful variety, and some looking strangely like green ice-crystals.

~ A dream of writer and physician Anna Kingsford, 1877

A Colorful Clue

THE WIZARD HELPED THE FAUN TO HIS HOOVES, touching him lightly on the brow with his staff. The staff broke the forest's forgetful spell over Deacon. He felt as though he had woken from one of those elusive, barely remembered dreams. All those inexplicable occurrences during his wandering through the woods were an impossibly confused puzzle of pictures.

"A wizard, you say?" Deacon looked at the old man in wonder, having never met a wizard. "What kind of wizard?"

"The first. I am the wizard upon which all wizards after have been styled, just as this enchanted forest is the forest upon which all after have been seeded from. I am also known as 'the wise old man' or 'the sage,' though I prefer not to be reminded of my age. Wizard is a far more romantic title, wouldn't you say? I am that."

"What are you doing here in the middle of the woods?" Deacon asked, wondering what he himself was doing in the middle of the woods.

"I had meant to ask you the same question. As for me, as I said I am a wizard. All wizards come from these woods.

Morgan le Fay lives in the Vale Perilous, nearer to the river. Merlin remains in the deepest, darkest part of the forest, trapped within an oak tree to this very day. Here there are white mages, blue mages, green mages, even time mages..."

A howl of wolves interrupted the wizard with a warning from just beyond the courtyard walls.

"Come, join me above the castle for a rest. You appear to need it."

The wizard led the exhausted faun back into the castle, where they proceeded through the barren halls. There was nothing and no one inside. There were no kings, queens, princes, or princesses. There were no royal furnishings, thrones, coats of arms, suits of armor, or magical mirrors. The great hall was greatly empty. The adjoining halls, bedchambers, kitchen, bathrooms, were all just as empty. The place was even empty of sound. Their footsteps made war on the silence, each one an explosion of echoes.

The two came upon a levitating, helical staircase within a wide, empty hall. The staircase reminded Deacon of the one from his lighthouse, without the walls of course. He followed the wizard carefully up, and up. He continued climbing the stairs, expecting to soon reach the top floor, but they never did. They continued straight through the roof of the castle, into the misty flowers of the storm, to the door of an oval shaped solar. The room floated over the castle like its own miniature, candle-lit moon.

Deacon followed the wizard inside. The room was brightly lit from a fire blazing within the cast iron stove. It was a comfortable stone chamber with a high, domed ceiling. The walls were decorated with elegant paintings of the surreal. Deacon recognized *The Wandering Moon* from his own collection. A detailed map of all those destinations

63

we dream hung above the stove. A long, straw bed lay along the wall.

The wizard sat down at a little table for two near an open window where stray storm flowers trickled in. He smoked from an immense corncob pipe. The bowl was so big it looked more like a cauldron for cooking than pipe for smoking. Deacon took a seat across from him at the table. He could hardly keep his horns up he was so tired. The wizard offered him a coffee, which he happily accepted.

"I've told you who I am," the wizard said as he placed a kettle over the fire. "I wonder who you are, all dressed for a voyage at sea, yet charting a course in the opposite direction. And a faun at that! Fauns are rare, even in these vast woods. There is a curly haired one, lives in the wood between worlds. Cheery, bookish chap. Likes a cup of tea. Do you know him?"

"No, I am not from these woods. I am the principal lighthouse keeper."

"A lighthouse keeper! How fascinating an occupation. I have never met a lighthouse keeper, let alone *the* lighthouse keeper. Tell me, do you find lighthouse keeping lonely?"

"Lonely, no. Isolated, yes. Loneliness and isolation are quite different. I have come across many a city-dwelling dreamer lonelier than the most remote of lighthouse keepers. I am friendlier with the seagulls than many are with their nearest neighbors. I do on occasion feel the need to venture from my outpost for news of the world, or friendly conversation, but not often."

"You've ventured far from your outpost. Tell me, what brings you to this forest of forests?"

"I am in pursuit of a deviant dreamer by the name of Rip Van Winkle. I have reason to believe he has been sleeping without interruption for months or more. Such a man may very well be the cause of this infernal storm. I set out many strange sunsets ago, sailing over stranger seas and into these strangest woods, but have seen no sign of him."

"You say you are a lighthouse keeper. Is it the duty of a lighthouse keeper to rescue, or simply to reveal? I doubt many lighthouse keepers would be willing to venture to the furthest reaches of Oblivion to liberate a lost dreamer. I do not know your full story, but it seems to me a most unusual one. I would have guessed you to be the hero in that story, just as I am the wizard. This forest is where the hero is tested, after all..."

Deacon laughed nervously as the wizard poured a scolding coffee that looked more like tar into a teacup. The scent alone had a stimulating effect.

"Sincerest of apologies to you, my most hospitable wizard, but there are no heroes on this side of the table. Just a dutiful, principal lighthouse keeper."

The wizard peered at the furry faun under his own furrier eyebrows, his ancient eyes twinkling with wisdom. Deacon peered back, his eyes twinkling with tears from the murderously strong coffee.

"Have you seen anything of this Rip Van Winkle?" Deacon asked. "Colonial. Yeoman. Mischievous, nostalgic fellow..."

"You are asking the wrong question. It seems to me time has passed this Rip Van Winkle by. Ask rather, where does one go to hide from time? Here, time passes the dreamer by in the blink of an eye, and they are whisked away to Wakefulness. Not so elsewhere."

"Where then, does one hide from time?"

"There are two safe havens from time: Yesterday and Tomorrow. Time will eventually track down Tomorrow.

Not so with Yesterday. We can return to Yesterday without the bother of time to overtake us."

"Interesting..." Deacon scratched his fur in contemplation. "The gentleman believed to be Rip Van Winkle just so happened to have been overserved on memories at the Sleeping Siren. He might have set sail for Yesterday, had he been in any condition to skillfully navigate a course there. The man could hardly stand."

"Destinations have a way of finding wayfaring souls on the Sea of Dreams. Look at you. Did you find me, and this castle, or was it the other way around?"

Deacon stroked his horns in perplexity. "I wonder what, or where, will find me next..."

"I think Yesterday will find you, and when it does you will find your Rip Van Winkle."

"I would rather home found me. This place reminds me of my own quarters. What I wouldn't give for my own seat in the clouds, a view of the endless sea instead of these endless woods. A pipe to smoke, a fire to poke, a beacon to tend..."

"No use tending a beacon in this tempest. Settle the storm, and you may settle down."

Deacon rubbed his tired eyes as he finished the coffee. Strong though it was, it stood no chance of keeping him awake. Some dreams must sleep, to awaken for someone else's night.

"How am I to reach Yesterday?" Deacon mumbled. "And where within that realm shall I search?"

"For the answer to those questions, we must seek out the glassblower. First, you must rest."

The wizard led Deacon to the straw bed. A moment after laying down, the faun found himself in a far more senseless Oblivion, one without wizards, wolves, and wights

...le slept as soundly as the sleeper he

...it here, a
fleeting
...ber

...TO THE SCENT OF RESIN AND FLOUR, ...of an empty stomach. He was pleased to find ...source of the smells emitting from the fresh coffee and scone awaiting him on his bedstand. The wizard sat in the same chair he had been in when Deacon went to sleep, smoking the same pipe. He had to have moved, but Deacon wasn't so sure.

"Good evening, lighthouse keeper. Your lookout is long past due!"

"Good evening, wizard. Thank you for the breakfast."

"I hope it suits you. The scone is lavender honey."

The scone tasted as if it had been baked by an all-powerful pastry chef with honey harvested from some wildflower nectar of the gods. That is to say, it was delicious. The faun devoured it, feeling instantly refreshed and ready for the next stage of his journey.

"Tell me, who is this glassblower?" Deacon asked as he washed down the scone. "Does he make windows? I should need a window or two replaced at the lighthouse after this storm."

"The glassblower is indeed a creator of windows, but they are not the sort one would expect to see in a lighthouse. His glass imitates life. You see, the glassblower is an artist."

"What type of glass then? Looking glass?"

"Stained glass, but of an uncommon variety. His glass is smeared with all those stunning views of life from behind closed eyes. He portrays the world from the perspective of the dreamer. You see, the typical dreamer remembers

hardly more than a few images — a portr[...]
landscape there. The glassblower captures those [...]
scenes in his work."

Deacon drank the last of his coffee, trying to remem[...]
his own fleeting night (or nights) before. He found he coul[...]
remember very little. Indeed, what he could remember was
only in pictures. A shadow here, a kiss there, a royal ball...

"How will the glassblower help us find Rip Van
Winkle?"

"The glassblower will form for us those visions from
Rip's dream. Those may provide a clue as to his
whereabouts."

"How does the glassblower know what Rip is
dreaming?"

"I don't know, and I don't think he knows. The
glassblower is a true artist, the instrument of some higher,
inventive power. He presents dream images in the same
way a plant presents flowers. Genuine works of art are an
expression of the subconscious mind. Most originate in the
deepest, darkest vales of these woods, shrouded in
imagination. No one has fully explored them, or
understands them. They remain a mystery to even me."

Deacon rose, polishing his horns to gold and shoeing his
hooves with silver for what he hoped was the last leg of his
journey. Soon, he and the wizard were out the door and
walking carefully back down the spiraling stairs. They
made their way out of the castle and through the ruinous
kingdom, back into the forest.

"Does the glassblower live in a castle like this one?"
Deacon asked.

"Certainly not. Artists cannot abide luxury. The
glassblower lives in an unassuming treehouse."

"A *treehouse*? Sounds mad."

"Every bit as mad as living in a lighthouse," the wizard pointed out. "Lighthouse keeping is for staying awake. Treehouse dwelling is for dreaming. That fact explains why only children, and the occasional artist, care for a treehouse. How easy it is to pass the time swaying like a cradle in the blowing branches, laughing, playing, talking over those fantasies of childhood. The treehouse itself is a distinctive sort of fantasy. It is a fort of fantasy, meant for the exchange of secret dreams, among other things."

"I hope the glassblower can exchange with us the secret dreams of Rip Van Winkle."

"He will have something for us. No one dreams for so long without inspiring a work of art."

THE TWO WEREN'T FAR INTO THE FOREST WHEN THEY came upon an area where the trees were larger and less crowded. Some of them were painted, with nooks carved out of the trunks like little shelters. There were far fewer dreamers, and they behaved differently. They were often alone, seeming more lucid and less wild. Most shied away from the pair as they walked by.

"You can tell these are artists," the wizard pointed out, "by the way they carry themselves. Observant, isolated, vulnerable. Some are also the most extreme risk-takers. Look!"

The wizard pointed up to what Deacon at first took to be the trembling limbs of a treetop. Looking closer, he saw it was actually a man painting the topmost leaves of one of the tallest trees. The daring artist painted with a gold so radiant it seemed as though the sun shone only on that portion of the tree. He was sprawled out like a monkey among the swaying branches. Deacon stopped to watch the spectacle, guessing the man might fall at any moment.

"Here we are, just up ahead." The wizard signaled back to Deacon, who hurried to catch up.

The wizard pointed to a wide, cavernous tree that towered above the others. The size and shape of it reminded Deacon of his own lighthouse. It was thickest at the bottom, narrowing on the way to the top where it was crowned with leaves of every color. The trunk was dotted with stained glass windows, each its own kaleidoscopic tree hollow. The green front door shone brightly against the amber-soaked bark framing it. There was a mailbox next to the door. The tree was unlike anything Deacon had ever seen, but the mailbox struck him as especially peculiar. Surely there were no letter carriers in that furthest back of back countries.

The wizard gave the door a rhythmic knock with his staff. It swung open as if by command. Deacon followed the wizard slowly in, surprised to find the care with which the entire tree had been hollowed out. A spiral staircase was all that was left, carved from the inside of the trunk itself. The wooden stairs led up and along the rim of the tree.

Deacon followed the wizard up, colorful shadows from the stained glass lighting their way. The two climbed and climbed, the stairs seeming to have no end, and the tree no top. They marched tiredly on until the spiral of the staircase finally started to shrink, the trunk closing in on each side. The sound of footsteps echoed from above.

The faun's legs were numb with exhaustion when they did finally reach the top, standing on a platform with a ladder leading up through an opening in the very top of the trunk. Climbing up and out of the tree, they found themselves on a circular treetop balcony with a sweeping view of the surrounding forest. They were well above the rest of the trees. At first, Deacon could hardly keep his eyes open the sky was so bright. And it wasn't that the sun was shining. The storm was still present, a drizzle of daisies in the air. It had just been so long since Deacon had been out of the woods, even the cloud cover was glaring.

After Deacon's eyes adjusted to the sky above, he looked down at the endless expanse of treetops below. A dusting of flowers covered the leaves, creating the illusion of a meadowland. Try as he might, Deacon could see no end to the forest in any direction. Then the wind returned. The lighthouse keeper in him was glad to have it back. He closed his eyes and received it like an old friend.

"What, sir, is your favorite color?" A shrill voice interrupted the reunion.

It was the glassblower, only he didn't look like a glassblower. At first glance, Deacon thought he wore a massively thick orange beard, but soon realized he was mistaken. The glassblower had no beard at all. He had orange fur, and it covered his face completely. The man had the head of an oversized red fox. Deacon tried not to stare.

"Sir? Did you not hear me? Your favorite color? What would that be?" the fox-man persisted.

"Ahem, excuse me. Yes, my favorite color..." Deacon thought a moment. "Now, I couldn't honestly say. It has been forever since someone asked me that question."

"I am truly sorry to hear that. You know, there is a real danger in not having a favorite color. We all had favorite colors once, as children. I have heard it said the moment you forget your favorite color is the moment you start growing old. We forget our senses along with color. First, we forget how to hear. Green rushes swaying in the wind. Bluegrass. White noise. Then comes smell. Vanilla. Cinnamon. Roses. Touch and taste go away together. Plump blueberry. Silky key lime pie. Colors cut across every possible method of perception—"

"—What is *your* favorite color?" the wizard interjected.

"Orange. Orange is truly the sixth sense. It is a feeling of joy, of fox fur."

"One might say orange is the reason we've come here." The wizard skillfully navigated the conversation, "we've lost the sunlight, as you may have noticed."

"Indeed, I have. I must admit I admired the storm, at first. One day, there was a flurry of sunflowers. They were beautiful, brightening the sky like thousands of teeny-tiny suns. Then came the paperwhite blossoms. Those things reek of goat piss, no offense to you, sir."

"None taken," Deacon responded. "I am only half goat."

"There seems no end to this storm and these falling flowers. Tell me wisest of wizards, what is the cause of it?"

"We believe the cause to be a delinquent dreamer by the name of Rip Van Winkle. This faun with me is the lighthouse keeper. He has come here in search of Rip, with hopes to end this storm, once and for all. I wonder if you may be able to help us? Blow us some glass, perhaps?"

"Rip Van Winkle... I recognize that name. I blew the glass of your dreamer weeks, no, months ago. Wait here, let me retrieve them from my collection."

The artist proceeded to a large, intricately carved hope chest on the far side of the treehouse. When opened, rays of gold and silver streamed out, as though it held some bottomless treasure. He rummaged around the chest, glass clanking and clinking all the while.

"Aha. Here it is," he announced, blowing a fine layer of dust from a small, stained glass window. Dust! Deacon wondered how long the glass had been in the chest. The glassblower handed the piece to the wizard, who carefully examined it.

The scene on the glass was that of a mountain meadow dotted with wildflowers. A jagged mountain perched high over the horizon, a river flowing down from its peak. It looked to be a summer day. The sky above was a piercing blue, the sun shining. A single cloud shaped like a rocking horse looked down on the scene. The landscape was so extraordinarily detailed, Deacon hadn't at first noticed the boy and girl who pranced through the meadow. He wondered who the two children were.

"I take that to be Rip Van Winkle." The wizard pointed a finger at the boy.

"That cannot be him," Deacon declared. "Rip Van Winkle is no boy."

"*Yesterday*, he was a boy. This stained glass holds a vision from the past. You can tell from the scent. Scent, emotion, and memory are all intertwined. Close your eyes and smell it."

Deacon closed his eyes and took a whiff. The scent triggered a memory from long ago, when he was an apprentice lighthouse keeper. He sat watch over the sea at sundown. He could see the current, clear as the glass-blowing fox in front of him. But the fragrant element of the flashback was not the sea, but the coming rain. Thunder grumbled in warning. It was the faun's first real storm, and it blew from Yesterday. The harshest storms always came from that way.

"So, Rip is in the past after all." The faun opened his eyes, "I wonder how he got there, and how I shall get there?"

"Yesterday is never far," the glassblower pointed out. "I'm sure the wizard will guide you. Please, take this stained glass with you as a souvenir. It would make for a fine addition to one of your lighthouse windows."

"Thank you. It will indeed."

Deacon knew just where to hang it. There was a porthole in his private library that faced Yesterday. The color of the sky in that direction was often faded and dreary. The stained glass rendition of the past would brighten the room, and his own remembrances.

———

THE TWO THANKED THE GLASSBLOWER AND SAID THEIR farewells. Deacon would have liked to enjoy the view for longer, but it seemed to him the wizard was in no mood for further delay. They proceeded down the long and winding treehouse trunk, back into the forest below. They hadn't traveled far when they encountered a fork in the trail, where the wizard stopped.

"This way leads to Yesterday." The wizard pointed his staff down a foggy, winding path.

"And the other way?" Deacon doubted himself out loud.

"The other way leads back to your lighthouse." The homeward path was straight and clear.

Deacon stood there, quietly trying to convince himself the road home was the right one. He had no idea what Yesterday had in store. It looked temperamental. He had of course once lived through Yesterday, but he had never returned there. He would rather return home.

The wizard sensed his apprehension.

"You know, I have no idea what class of dream a lighthouse keeper is. Are you the innocent or the outlaw? The lover or the leaver? The hero or the coward? If you happened to be the hero, I would say here is the part of the hero's journey where he is truly tested. You have already heard your call, acted on your adventure, and crossed the threshold. Now for the ordeal..."

"*Now* for the ordeal? How would you characterize my misadventures in the woods? From what I remember, that was quite the ordeal!" Deacon's voice rose. He was in no mood for ordeals. He was in the mood for idleness. Sitting, watching with his beacon. A tremendous cup of tea. An equally tremendous book. "And I must say, this hero talk has me vexed. I am no hero. The great shadow would have devoured me were it not for you. I cowered in fear at first sight of it. What if I should encounter it again? What was that infernal shadow, anyway?"

"The shadow pursuing you was a simple one, like all of the other shadows in these parts, only much larger. It is that dark, dreamful doppelganger our waking self."

"A shadow of such proportions must be cast by a sizably valiant character."

"Indeed. The shadow was your own."

Deacon stood open-mouthed as he tried to make sense of the wizard's revelation. He vaguely remembered the mirror at the riverside and the phantom emerging from it. Had it at first looked like him? Perhaps, but only for a moment.

"Here we find ourselves in the midst of this great forest, surrounded by even greater forests," Deacon pointed out, frustrated. "The road to Yesterday must be impossibly long. How far must I travel down the path until I reach it?"

"The distance to Yesterday is not measured in miles. It is measured in thoughts. Your mind takes you there faster than your feet. Rip is no more than a notion down the trail."

"How will I know it when I see it? What does it look like?"

"You will know it. Yesterday looks like a long forgotten memory."

Deacon looked down the trail, contemplating the past, and Rip. As he did, it seemed to him the path changed. Stray rays of sunlight pierced the fog. The trees on either side became less crowded. The trail widened as it sloped higher, appearing to lead up and out of the woods. The way looked hopeful. So was Deacon.

"Farewell, wizard. I will dress my lighthouse window in this stained glass, should I ever return. I will think of you and these woods when the light shines through it, should it ever return."

"You shall return, and so shall the light. Until we meet again, may your own light never grow dim, and your shadow never grow less!"

Deacon started down the path to the past. He hadn't traveled far when he heard a rustle in the tall, thick rushes along the trail. They were blowing in the wind, their swaying sound provoking a long forgotten memory. He looked at them, finally remembering his favorite color. Green.

He knew then he had arrived in Yesterday.

There is a dream which I can cause as often as I like, as it were experimentally. If in the evening I eat anchovies, olives, or other strongly salted foods, I become thirsty at night, whereupon I waken. The awakening, however, is preceded by a dream, which each time has the same content, namely, that I am drinking. I quaff water in long draughts, it tastes as sweet as only a cool drink can taste when one's throat is parched, and then I awake and have an actual desire to drink. The occasion for this dream is thirst, which I perceive when I awake. The wish to drink originates from this sensation, and the dream shows me this wish as fulfilled.

The content of the dream is thus the fulfilment of a wish.

∼ Sigmund Freud, founder of psychoanalysis, 1899

Forfeits

The trail led Deacon out of the enchanted forest and into an ordinary one. Restless shadows of dreamers were replaced with those of motionless trees. There was no sign of anyone, dreaming or not. The odd squirrel was the faun's only companion as he walked on. He was pleased to have left Oblivion, yet remained cautiously optimistic at the idea of Yesterday.

"Surely, the past will be more predictable," he supposed. "After all, it has already happened."

How wrong he was.

The path steepened as it rose higher, so that walking gradually turned to climbing. He had been climbing only a little while when, to his relief, he reached a flat, grassy ridge. Relief turned to disbelief as he looked into the distance and realized he was halfway up a mountainside — the Catskills. Looking down, he saw the thin blue string of Hudson River slicing through the valley. Smoke rose from houses hidden in the woods. He sat down on a boulder to rest and take in the view. He had just started to whistle when he was interrupted.

"Shh!" came a voice from the trees behind him.

Deacon rose from the rock in surprise. He looked around but saw no one.

"Must have been a bird," Deacon guessed out loud.

"SHHHHHHH!" the voice hissed louder.

Deacon got a good look at the tree where the voice came from and walked carefully toward it. He was nearly there when a scraggly little boy no older than ten or eleven leapt out from behind the trunk. He was dressed in a raggedy undershirt and ripped trousers, muddy feet peeking out of his torn pant legs. Long, unkempt rolls of hair spilled out from under his corn husk hat. He wore a look of surprise on his freckled face, mouth open wide as could be, eyes even wider.

"Wh... What are you?" the boy asked.

"I am the lighthouse keeper," Deacon replied, realizing as he did that the boy was not asking *who* he was, but *what* he was. "I am also a faun. I suppose you have never met a faun, have you?"

"No. What is a faun?" The boy came closer, staring all the time at Deacon's horns.

"A faun is half-human, half-goat. See these hairy legs, and these hooves," Deacon pointed out. "What do you think of my horns? Have you ever seen such an odd, curly bone?"

"No, sirree! May I please touch your horns?"

Deacon knelt before the boy, who gently pet his horns, smiling with fascination.

"Where do you live?" the boy asked.

"You ask many questions little one! I will allow you this last one, before I ask you a few of my own. I live in a lighthouse, quite far from here."

"A lighthouse! I should like to visit a lighthouse. I have never been to the sea."

"No? Perhaps a visit can be arranged. Come now, I have told you all about me. What about you? Tell me boy, who are you?"

"Name is Rip. Rip Van Winkle. Pleasure to meet you, sir."

The boy held his hand out. Deacon shook it in disbelief. Finally, here was *the* Rip Van Winkle, the object of Deacon's long, arduous journey. Did Rip realize he was dreaming? It seemed not, but there was no way to be certain. Deacon didn't know what to do or say. He hadn't planned for the actual encounter, and although he had been told Rip would be a child, he was still surprised. He was surprised once more by a shriek of laughter from the trail.

"Mister goat-man, HIDE!" Rip pulled Deacon down by the hand. The two ducked behind the tree, looking back toward the trail.

"Who are we hiding from?" Deacon whispered.

"Rosie. She's *IT*. We're playing hide-and-seek."

"BOO!" the voice of a girl startled them from behind. She looked to be the same age as Rip, though far cleaner. She wore a white calico dress dotted with daisies. It was still sprinkling wildflowers, making the dress a sort of camouflage. Her heart-shaped face was flushed from running, making her blonde hair and robin egg blue eyes all the brighter.

"RUN!" Rip hollered as he hurried back toward the trail with Deacon close behind.

Rosie chased after them. Running along the trail, they were soon joined by more children. Some of them glanced curiously at the faun, but none seemed to mind that he had joined in the fun. Deacon galloped along with the others, bringing up the rear. Rosie was close behind. They all laughed and sang as they raced along, as children will in the midst of a game.

The trail rose steeply at its end. One by one, they reached the hilly boundary of the woods, where they looked out upon a meadow of wildflowers. Deacon recognized the scene from the stained glass. It was unmistakably the same. The only difference was the flowers. They rose straight from the soil itself, soaring into the sky before drifting off in different directions. The sky above was the clearest blue, without even a dusting of cloud cover. Deacon realized then that the meadow was the eye of the strange storm that had been raging for so long.

The sight of the meadow sent the children into a frenzy. Hoots and hollers echoed from the mountainside as they ran and rolled through the endless flowers. The first ever playgrounds were meadows, and the children treated that one accordingly. Deacon was (uncharacteristically) playful as the rest. The flower petals felt wonderful below his hooves, a welcome change from the rocky trails. He galloped about, happy for his adventure to be over, or so he thought.

Deacon kept a close eye on Rip, which meant keeping a close eye on Rosie. The two were never far apart. She did finally catch him. Tackling him from behind, the two drowned in a pile of poppies. Thinking Rip disappeared again, Deacon rushed over to find the pair laying on their backs, looking up at the floating flowers. Deacon lay down with them.

The faun gazed up at some newly arrived clouds congregating over the field. They were the first benign clouds he had seen in what seemed like forever. Like the children, his imagination was unleashed on the sky. In the clouds, he saw rocking horses rocking, dragons belching forth white flames, and whole celestial kingdoms floating by. Further off in the distance, just over the mountaintop where the day met night, curvy pink clouds swung their hips like hula dancers.

"We should play a game!" Rosie suggested as she leapt up.

"A game, of course! What game?" Rip asked excitedly.

"Forfeits!"

Forfeits was a once popular game, sadly forgotten today. It was often played by children of the colonial era. The game was played with any number of players. A personal item or prize, known as a "forfeit" was offered up by each player and returned on the completion of some task or feat. Forfeits could be anything: small gifts, ornaments, toys. The process of redeeming the forfeit was the real fun in the game. One player who had been selected judge would sit in a chair, while another held the forfeit over the judge's head, saying, "Heavy, heavy, what hangs over thy head?" The judge would then ask, "Fine or superfine?" to which the other would respond, "Fine," if the owner is a boy, or, "Superfine," if a girl, adding, "What shall the owner do to redeem it?" The judge would then command the owner to do some exciting or ridiculous feat to reclaim his property.

Deacon joined the children as they exchanged forfeits. There were trinkets, coins, candy, and of course flowers. Rip offered up his corn husk hat. Rosie gave a tiny toy toad. Deacon put forth his stained glass. The oldest of the boys was selected judge and sat upon a tree stump on the outskirts of the meadow. Deacon and the children circled around him.

The judge closed his eyes. The children joined together and sifted through the prizes. Rip's hat was selected as the first forfeit. Rosie held the mangy thing over the judge's head.

"Heavy, heavy hangs over thy poor head," Rosie pronounced.

"Fine or superfine?" the judge asked.

"Fine," Rosie smiled at Rip. "What shall the owner do to redeem his property?"

The judge thought a few seconds before raising his hand in command.

"Bow to the wittiest, kneel to the prettiest, and kiss the one that he loves best."

The children cheered with excitement. The verdict was a brilliant combination of truth and dare. Rip must confess his love, and kiss her while he was at it. He stepped forward.

"The wittiest cannot be denied," Rip bowed to the judge. The children nodded their heads in hurried agreement, eager for his next move.

"Nor can the prettiest," he kneeled to a blushing Rosie, taking her by the hand. The storm intensified with the moment. "As for the one I love best," he kissed her on the hand. "I kneel in service before her majesty, the queen consort of these Catskills, Rosie O'Ryan."

The children roared. Rosie curtsied. The judge crowned her with a circlet of saffron petals. Rip was crowned with his corn husk hat, having successfully earned it back.

Deacon nervously watched the coronation. He was ready to wake Rip and go home, but felt as though something was wrong. There was more to Rip than met the eye. At times, he sounded more man than boy. Rip was not the least bit shy in his confession of love for Rosie, and did so in front of everyone. Such a declaration struck Deacon as much too bold for a child.

The children played on, alternating judge every so often. Eventually, Rip was appointed judge. He sat on the tree stump and closed his yes. The children selected Deacon's stained glass as forfeit. Rosie held the stained glass over Rip's head. Deacon watched and waited, wondering what Rip would command of him to win back the prize.

"Heavy, heavy hangs over thy poor head," Rosie chanted, holding the stained glass. It filtered the blue sky above into a colorful halo upon Rip's hat.

"Fine or superfine?" Rip's eyes popped open, staring straight at Deacon, as though he knew it were the stained glass.

"Fine," she answered. It sounded suspiciously like "faun" to Deacon.

"What shall the owner do to redeem his property?"

Rip rose from the tree stump, marching slowly toward Deacon.

"Answer me one question," he stopped in front of the faun. "What are you doing here?"

Deacon was caught completely off guard. Rip looked and sounded quite serious, for a boy. Was the question part of the game? Was it a truth he must tell to win back the stained glass? And could he even tell the truth — that this was all the past, the children all memories? He stood there dumbfounded, unsure of what to say, or do.

"Well, what *are* you doing here?" Rip's voice rose. "Answer the question to win back your forfeit!" The children crowded closer around the faun, squinting with suspicious eyes as if they were only then just noticing him. Deacon had to say something.

"I am not here to win back the forfeit. I am here for your forfeit, Rip Van Winkle. This game, these flowers, you, me, it is all a dream of long ago. And you have been dreaming for far too long. I have come to wake you, to take you home, back to the morning, where you belong."

The children backed away in stunned silence. None had known they were bygone apparitions. Where we dream, the past is as unknowing as the future, and often indistinguishable from the present. Rip and Rosie were the only two to stand their ground in front of Deacon. Rosie sneered at him, clearly dissatisfied with his explanation. Rip tossed the stained glass over his shoulder, where it disappeared in a bed of flowers.

The confused silence lasted only a moment. Then there was chaos. Deacon's revelation invited time from the past to the present in just a few tumultuous moments. The eye of the storm closed. The winds rose. The mountains crumbled into the Sea of Dreams. The meadow remained, but was transformed into a cliff overlooking the sea. The children changed. Most simply aged. Others scattered or disappeared entirely.

Rosie and Rip remained unchanged, but not unmoving. They dashed hand in hand through the meadow to the cliff's edge. Deacon chased after them. By the time he reached them, the storm had settled down, with the exception of the winds, which blew in irregular and oftentimes tremendous gusts.

"Where are you going?" Deacon shouted over the wind.

"I'm going to sleep," Rip matter-of-factly countered.

"You can't stay here," Deacon declared.

"OF COURSE I CAN!" Rip yelled.

Suddenly the wind stopped, and the wildflowers with it. They no longer rose from the meadow, soaring up into the stormy sky. Rip stooped over and picked one. It was a puffy white dandelion. He held it up for the faun to see.

"Did you know dandelions were flowers? This one here

is magic. There is no magic where I come from. There are no enchantments, or sorcerers to cast them. Where I come from, there is only disenchantment. Time there is a merciless arrow. Once yesterday has passed, there is no returning. Not so here. Here, you need only travel to Yesterday. And magic is real, if only you can find it."

"Magic is within us all, waking or sleeping," Deacon explained.

"Is that so?" Rip looked at Rosie. "There is far more evidence for it while asleep."

"In dreams, magic comes with a price."

"Does it? I've not a shilling to pay, yet here I am."

"It does," Deacon reasoned. "We deal in strange currencies here. Time is one."

"Perhaps, though a debt to time never comes due in the past."

"Can you not see? Time has already passed you by!" Deacon shouted in frustration. "It has passed you by here in this dominion of dreams, and it has passed you by in your wakeful world! Your debt here will be paid to time, with age!"

"So, you have come to save me from myself, from the creeping hands of a clock?

"I have. Surrender to time, and me!" Deacon took a step toward Rip.

"Go away, you beastly goat!" Rosie cried as she charged forward, kicking Deacon in the shins. "Shoo! Leave us alone!"

Deacon backed away.

"One last bit of magic before I wake," Rip declared.

The winds rose one last time, blowing the hat from Rip's head. It sailed over the cliff's edge and into the sea far below. Rip closed his eyes, long hair blowing wildly. He held the dandelion up, made a silent wish, and blew the little white seeds from the bulb.

What did he wish?

Rip wished never to wake. The wish came true not because the dandelion was some magic talisman, or because Rip was some powerful magician. It came true because Rip knew something no one else did. He knew that dreams were oftentimes no more than wishes yet to come true. The act of the wishing for an endless sleep formed a new and endless dream.

The moment Rip dropped the dandelion stem, the cliff where he stood collapsed into the sea. Rip made no attempt to save himself. He fell straight down without a whisper. The waves roared to greet the mass of rock, dust, and dream. Rosie dove off the cliff after him. Unlike Rip, she never hit the water. Instead, she flew low over it into the distance, toward Wakefulness. It wasn't long before she was out of sight.

Deacon was left alone on the cliff's edge. He looked hopelessly into the sea for some sign of Rip, but there was no trace of him. The boy was gone, sunk to the unfathomable depths of the subconscious, among all those undiscovered mysteries of the mind. Deacon wondered to himself if that was where Rip was always destined to be. After all, Rip was a mystery himself, still unsolved for the time being.

Deacon looked up from the sea to the sky. He had never seen a night so clear. The wildflowers were all gone, having fallen to the ground and faded away. Stars blinked back to life, shooting here and there in celebration of the unobstructed ether. They shone down brighter than before, as if making up for lost time. The moon joined them, rising slowly over the horizon, a wistful smile on its face. All was returned to normal in the night.

Deacon peered out over the sea like the lighthouse keeper he was. Intentional dreamers walked on water to somewhere. Stray dreamers walked on air to nowhere. Adrift sailboats dotted the waves. He was pleased at the sight of the night, but how dark it all seemed.

He must return home, for the sea was in need of navigating. A beacon would help.

The Wakeful Whereabouts of
Rip Van Winkle

"I HAD THE STRANGEST DREAM LAST NIGHT..."

A grown-up Rosie O'Ryan explained over breakfast one cold, colonial morning. She was grown-up because she had woken up. Allow us to return to the wakeful world for a brief, explanatory interlude concerning the whereabouts of Rip Van Winkle.

Her wakeful name was not Rosie O'Ryan, but Mrs. Rose Livingston. She sat in the dining room of her manor house, at the head of a long and luxuriously set table. She was joined by a household nurse on one side, and a baby boy (her son) on the other. Servants were busy all around, pouring fresh coffee, serving johnny cakes, saturating johnny cakes in butter-syrup, tidying up this or that. The lord of the manor was away.

"A Dream! Do tell it. Dreams make for the most interesting stories," said the nurse.

"I was back home, only not this home. I was back in the Catskills, in that hamlet of my girlhood. It has been so many years since I've been back, I hardly recognized it. And the dream itself *was* years ago. I was well in the past, still just the littlest girl."

"Is that so? I should like to be a girl again. Whatever did you do?"

Rose stared out the dining room window, trying to recall the dream. She noticed the first snowflakes from the approaching blizzard drifting down in beautiful warning. The falling snow helped her to remember the falling flowers.

"We played. I was on the mountainside, in a meadow where the children of the village used to gather. It was the most colorful scene. There were the brightest reds, blues, oranges, pinks, and purples everywhere, above and below. The color was from the flowers. They sailed through the air in every direction, no different than the snowflakes outside.

"How wonderful it must be to dream in such colors. My dreams are black and white."

The nurse was interrupted by an outburst from the baby. She plucked him from his high chair, swaying and cooing him to no avail. A servant rushed to her rescue, feeding the boy bacon bits and milk. Rose watched the scene with unease. She would have preferred to care for her son herself, but her husband was a man of high society. He would not allow anything of the sort. The baby quieted, and Rose continued.

"Old friends were there with me, all running this way and that. Some I recognized. Others not. Many are now long dead. There was a particular boy there..."

"A *particular* boy, you say? Mrs. Livingston, this dream has the makings of a scandal! Reuniting with long-lost lovers in the middle of the night, are we? But then, don't we all? It is one of those facts of life that no one will confess to. Tell me, who was this *particular* boy? Your secret is safe with me."

"He was the only son of a nearby farmer. We wandered the wild woods and winding country roads together as children. We were always making mischief of some sort. He was poor, but rich in spirit. He was one of those wakeful dreamers, always playing at make-believe, hiding deep within the woods, fantasizing over the unimaginable."

Rose sipped her coffee, watching the then fast-falling snow. The talk of childhood made her want to dash outside and play in it. Unfortunately, a woman of her stature was not to play in the snow, or anywhere. She must be a *good wife*, abiding by that strict code of ethics which governed female life in the colonies. She must act her class.

"Where was I?" Rose continued, "Oh yes, the meadow. In the dream, we were playing a game we often played — heavy, heavy hangs over thy head. The *particular* boy knelt before me and confessed his undying love. Then, there was a great commotion. Everything changed. The whole forest was uprooted. The mountain fell away. The children disappeared. Myself, the particular boy, and a most curious faun were the only ones remaining."

"I've heard it told fauns represent an other-worldly magic, or a desire to believe in magic," the nurse pointed out.

"I am certain there was talk of magic in the dream, though I can't recall exactly what was said on the subject. Shortly after the faun arrived, the dream dissolved all around us. All of a sudden, we were on the edge of a high cliff overlooking an immense ocean. The particular boy fell into it. I fell after him, then flew away, all the way to this morning."

"This *particular* boy, what was his name?"

"Rip," Rose said softly. "Rip Van Winkle."

"Rip Van Winkle? I'm sure I recognize that name from somewhere. Excuse me a moment missus," the nurse flagged down a servant. "Would you fetch the news for us?"

The servant agreed, soon returning with a stack of newspapers. The nurse sifted through them, before finding the one she was looking for.

"I knew I recognized that name. What a strange, sad coincidence this is. I am sorry to say you should read this." The nurse handed Rose a single page from the obituaries. Rose recognized his name at the top of the page.

RIP VAN WINKLE
1745 - 1770

DECLARED DEAD AFTER FIRST REPORTED MISSING IN *Catskills, 1769, leaving a wife to mourn the sad loss. Last seen at King George Inn, where he was well-liked by all. His death cast a quite a gloom over the friendly village. Preceded in death by father, Pappy Van Winkle.*

ROSE HELD THE NEWSPAPER UP LONG AFTER SHE'D finished reading to conceal the tears.

LATER THAT NIGHT, THE SAME SNOW FELL UPON THE village of Catskills. It was piling high outside the King George Inn, where a sizeable crowd was gathered. The inn was busiest in the early winter months. Just after the harvest, the farmers of the area had less work to do in the fields. They escaped from tedious days, restless children, and exasperated wives, joining together with others who suffered from the same domestic vexations.

Rip Van Winkle was the topic of discussion that night due to the fact his obituary had just been published. The King George Inn was exuberant at having been mentioned in print. The patrons speculated as to the author of the obituary, and the whereabouts of Rip, who by that time had been missing for over a year.

"Poor Rip. First gone missing, now declared dead. God rest his soul, wherever it is..."

"Better dead than alive in a bed next to that succubus, Dame Van Winkle. No doubt she authored the obituary..."

"Aye, *a wife to mourn the sad loss!*" The whole inn laughed together.

"Rip remains quite the mystery. I wonder wherever he got off to that night?"

A group of patrons went round a long table, each speculating as to Rip's fate.

"Gone mad in my own humble opinion," grumbled an old codger. "Rip always had an odd way about him. Been wandering those haunted woods up in the mountains since he was just a lad. Probably walked himself straight off a cliff, or into a river."

"I'd say scalped to death by Injuns more likely," suggested a fur trader. "Mohawk braves wandering about them woods that same time he went missing last year. I saw em."

"I say that raw-boned rum dubber made a meal for a family of black bears," proprietor Nicholas Vedder suggested as he left another round of drinks. "That was nearer to hibernation season when he went missing. Those woods would've been crawling with black bears looking to fatten up for the winter. Hope it was quick and painless for him."

The blizzard interrupted their theorizing. It came in through the front door, which swung wildly open from the wind and snow. All leapt nervously from their seats, the thought of black bears fresh in their minds. The patrons sat back down when they realized it was a man. The new guest was a fur-draped farmer by the name of Vance Van Dijk, long-time friend of Rip.

"Vance, come sit with us a few minutes. Spare us some light from that dazzling mind. We were just now discussing the disappearance, and recent death pronunciation, of one Rip Van Winkle. Word has it you had a few, or more than a few, libations with Rip the night he went missing."

Vance hung his coat by the door and proceeded to sit with the group.

"Rye whiskey for me tonight." He signaled to Vedder. "Too drafty for draft."

The group waited with polite patience until the whiskey was served to begin their questioning.

"Tell us Vance, in what condition was Van Winkle on that fateful evening?"

"I've told you this tale how many times? I'll tell it again, hoping against hope it will be the last."

Vance took a healthy swig of whiskey.

"Rip was drunk as Dionysus. Pour soul was numbing himself from the incessant heckling of Dame Van Winkle, and his unfortunate lot in life. Isn't that the reason we're all here? I expect some of us would prefer to be lost in the wilderness than to return home tonight!"

The inn laughed in wholehearted agreement. They toasted with glasses, drank glasses, dropped glasses, and ordered more glasses. Vedder hauled a bundle of fresh wood to the fire. They would need it. The night was growing colder, and no one would be leaving, not anytime soon. The snow was falling too hard, and looked too beautiful from the inside.

"Yes, but we already know of his inebriated state," a clearly inebriated patron persisted. "Not a soul departs from this place after midnight in temperate fashion. Tell us instead what his sober state of mind was. What was he speaking of in your conversation? Where was his head?"

Vance downed his whiskey, tired of the same line of questioning he'd heard dozens of times from these same men. Vedder brought him another whiskey. He sipped that one more mindfully, staring into the fire. His imagination formed the shapes of men in the flames, which roared from the fresh fuel. It reminded of him of hell, and Rip burning alive in it.

"Rip's body was sitting here, as real as all of you, but his head was somewhere else entirely. I think it was in the past. Hard to blame him. His present was a hardship, his future hopeless."

"That so? I hear he was out on the prowl for his cow?"

"Aye. That cow was worth more than his house. He wasn't *exactly* looking for it. Say rather, it was looking for him. And it found him. It waddled to the front door of this very inn."

"What was the last thing you said to him?"

"I don't recall, nor would Rip. He was bollixed beyond all comprehension. Vedder lent him a lantern for the trip home, and the odd couple disappeared down the road. Saw them fade into the night with mine own two eyes."

"The last two eyes that ever saw him," noted one.

"Unless Dame Van Winkle butchered him," corrected another.

Laughs sounded from throughout the Inn.

"Where is the venerated Dame Van Winkle these days, anyway?"

———

SHE WAS AT HOME.

The newly declared widow sat sipping a celebratory sherry in Rip's favorite armchair. She was delighted at the pronouncement of his death. The hearth blazed brightly, working hard to fend off the snow and cold outside. Her only friend, a reticent spinster from the village, joined her. The two talked about the long-lost, newly deceased Rip Van Winkle.

"The cow came home, but Rip never did?" the spinster questioned.

"Yes, thank the lord above. If you had asked me who I would rather have return home that night or any night, the cow or Rip, I would absolutely have chosen the cow," Dame Van Winkle giggled. "The cow is a far more industrious beast."

"Whatever do you think happened to him?" the spinster needled. "I've heard various theories around town. Tales of malice and murder linger about the inn. Do you believe any to be true?"

"Rip had the queerest nature. I have no doubt the way in which he died was as strange as the life he lived. My favorite yarn on the subject of his demise is the one with ghosts. Have you heard that one? The children of the village tell it, or so I've been told."

"No, but I do love a ghost story. And this night is suitable for one."

It was indeed one of those dark and stormy nights you're always hearing about, the perfect conditions for a ghost story. The snowfall was erratic, with stray patches of it creeping through the woods like roaming bands of spirits. Snowy, skeletal trees came to life, flailing crazily in the wind. None dared venture into the wilderness that night.

"The story starts quite realistically. Rip gets himself drunk as a monkey at the King George Inn. He wanders up into the woods on the mountainside. As you may know, those woods are said to be haunted by the long-dead crew of Henry Hudson's ship, the *Half Moon*. Captain Hudson sailed far down the river in search of a passage to the Orient. Too far. His ship was eventually stranded in ice. He and the crew spent a miserable winter aboard, barely able to survive. In the spring, Hudson wanted to continue up the river. His crew, having been trapped through the hard winter, mutinied. They set Hudson, his son, and several of their loyalists adrift. The marooned explorers were never seen again."

The spinster was of an especially faint-hearted nature. She sipped her tea for comfort, looking anxiously out the window for some sign of Hudson and his ghost crew. The wind howled at her, the snow piling high against the windows.

"No one knows what happened to Hudson and his men. Legend has it their spirits inhabit the mountainside. It is said they drink a mystical liquor and play at nine-pins. They say if you look far up into the mountains on a clear night, you can see a fire from their gathering. They say you can hear the sound of a nine-pin ball like thunder echoing through the whole valley."

"And Rip had joined in their spectral jubilee?" the spinster asked.

"So they say. For me, it is a believable tale. Rip would have preferred to waste away the rest of eternity playing at games, drinking himself to oblivion, hiding away from the responsibilities of society up there in the mountains with no one to reach him."

A scratching sounded at the door. The spinster rose in alarm.

"Sit down," Dame commanded as she finished her sherry. "It is only that infernal mutt of his. Wolf is his name, and a proper one at that. A wolf would be easier to train. That dog is good for nothing but waste collection. I wish Rip had taken him with him, wherever he went."

Dame went to the kitchen, gathering some scraps from the table. She opened the door and launched the bits of leftovers into the snow, before slamming it in the shivering, starving dog's face. Wolf quickly devoured everything. He then bound off through the tall mounds of snow into the trees. He was returning to his master.

WOLF FOLLOWED A HARDLY NOTICEABLE DEER PATH UP and up, higher onto the mountainside, deeper into the darkness of the woods. The snow was deep and the trees dense, but he moved fast. He moved even faster across the meadow. The top layer of snow there was hard enough to trot on. An owl hooted in hello as he re-entered the forest, sliding across an icy creek, before hopping up the bank. He wound this way and that around the trees, never stopping, not for a sniff. He knew that he must hurry, for the frost-fiends hunt in the dead of night.

The snow stopped as Wolf neared his destination. Gripped with cold, all was eerily still in the faraway forest. The woods were a motionless maze of ivory. White pines stood all around like massive, skyward-stabbing icicles, their frozen-stiff branches crackling in agony.

Wolf came upon the hollowed out oak tree he called home. It was buried in snow drifts, looking more igloo than tree. The dog dug a narrow entryway through the snow into the tree. Inside was a warm welcome from his cold trek through the woods. It was dry as ever, without a flake of snow to be found. Not a breath of winter wind breached the timeless trunk. The moss-covered ground was soft and snug. Lichen crept up the still-sleeping Rip Van Winkle's hands and into his shirtsleeve, so that he was starting to look more plant than person.

Wolf shook the snow off his coat and readied himself for bed. He wagged his tail in greeting as he licked the whiskers of his now bushy-bearded master, before snuggling into his lap. Rip didn't move a muscle. A foghorn wouldn't have woken him. He was lost in the deepest of dream-seas, and wouldn't rise from those depths for many years to come.

An Unexpected Story

BACK TO SLEEP.

After the boy Rip was swallowed in the Sea of Dreams, all returned to normal. The wind fell to a whisper. The waves settled to a ripple. The flowers returned to the earth, either sinking into the sea or sprouting from the ground. Children dreamed of mothers and monsters, adolescents of falling and flying, adults of Yesterday and Tomorrow.

The dreaded storm passed out of sight and mind, but it was not without consequence. Low-lying islands like Tír na nÓg, Hawaiki, and Avalon were overcome by the rising sea, never to be dreamed of again. Watered from the colorful rains, every enchanted forest grew lush and tall. Many a dreamer was lost or castaway, leading to a general anxiety and instability in the waking world, especially within the British colonies of America. There, a restless population of dreamers sought to establish their rightful place in the world through revolution.

Deacon was pleased to return to his routine at the lighthouse. He passed the time in regimented bliss, trimming wicks, washing windows, watching the water. He documented meteorological conditions within his lighthouse diary. He documented poems within his personal diary. He shone his navigational beacon upon the deepest and darkest of dream-seas, aiding the occasional errant dreamer. He did all those curious and monotonous jobs of a lighthouse keeper, and he was happy.

There was one aspect of Deacon's routine that had changed since his adventure — he'd taken up sailing. He promised himself he would in those first rapturous moments of his navigating the strange seas to Oblivion. With the help of a lucid-dreaming shipbuilder, he built for himself a simple and sturdy sloop.

One day, Deacon set forth on his new boat for a fishing excursion. As you may recall, the faun was an unconventional fisherman. He fished not for fish, but secrets. He owed a worthy secret to the mermaid in exchange for the information she had provided him concerning Rip's whereabouts.

Deacon circled his little island, never more than a stone's throw from shore, fishing for secrets all the livelong day. He'd caught some interesting ones. An age-old message in a bottle disclosed all those long-lost Eleusinian passwords. Secret tongues spoke of unconfessed sins on the sea breeze. He'd used his net to wrangle in long-hidden desires, fetishes, and infidelities. He caught more lies than anything. As usual, the waters were stocked with lies. Lies are like common carp in the Sea of Dreams — easy to catch but of little worth.

"Have you caught a secret worth revealing?" the mermaid asked, rising from the sea.

"No, not today I'm afraid."

"Bugger." The mermaid splashed him with her tail as she dove under the waves.

Deacon fished until the first stars of a clear night signaled him back to shore. Duty called with the darkening sky. He was turning his boat toward the dock when out of the corner of his eye, he spied a dot on the horizon. The dot caught his eye because it didn't come from Wakefulness, where the usual sea-traffic of dreamers came from. The dot came from Tomorrow.

Taking out his spyglass for a closer look, he saw it was a single-masted cutter gliding speedily over the waves in his direction. Deacon recognized the ship. It was a nautical library, her captain a seafaring librarian. The ship was delivering books to the lighthouse.

Maritime law requires all lighthouses to be regularly stocked with a fresh supply of books. The books delivered on that day were no ordinary books. Coming from Tomorrow, they were books that had yet to be written.

"Good evening, principal lighthouse keeper," the librarian-sailor greeted, fuzzy-hair from the sea wind blown over his beady, bespectacled eyes. He looked more librarian than sailor.

"Good evening, librarian," Deacon responded as he pulled his boat alongside the librarian's, mooring the two together before hopping excitedly over. Deacon was pleased to find the boat littered with books of every shape and size. He was in dire need of new reading material.

"Come, and take choice of all my library, and so beguile thy sorrow!" The Shakespeare quote was the librarian's way of inviting Deacon aboard for books. He often quoted Shakespeare.

"Thank you, and just in time. Voltaire has spent my appetite for anything remotely non-fictional. What do you have in the genre of literary fiction, even fantasy? I should like an escape from this lighthouse, if only in my mind."

"Ah, we have plenty. Imaginations have been radicalized in the realm of Tomorrow."

"That so? Why?"

"I suspect all the fantasizing is counterbalancing the dehumanizing effects of urbanization and industrialization. It is difficult for one to find meaning in a modern society. Perhaps the less meaning we find in our waking lives, the more we seek in dreams."

"That so..." Deacon mumbled as he picked through the piles of books. He wondered how the librarian steered the boat with such a mess scattered about.

"Look over there, near the wheel," the librarian directed.

Deacon waded through the books to the wheel, where there sat a tall stack of poetry. He grabbed something from Robert Burns because it was Robert Burns. *Rime of the Ancient Mariner* captured his heart with the title alone. *Songs of Experience* by William Blake was a must. Blake was a regular at the Sleeping Siren, often indulging in the most fantastical of concoctions. Deacon had drunk with William on a handful of memorable occasions, the full retelling of which would consume the remaining pages of this book.

A disproportionate amount of verse in hand, Deacon waded his way to the stern where he sought to diversify his collection. There he happened upon a treasure-trove of the finest in future fiction. *Faust. Ivanhoe. Sense and Sensibility. Pride and Prejudice.* The discovery of *Frankenstein* excited him so much, he found he couldn't get off the boat and back into his lighthouse fast enough to read it.

He was doing just that and had one hoof over the side of the boat, when another book grabbed hold of his attention like a voluminous vise. It was a worn and faded novel which lay on the gunwale near to where he was about to step off the boat. Deacon thought it strange he hadn't noticed it when he stepped on the boat. He stared at the title in disbelief.

Rip Van Winkle

Washington Irving

DEACON DROPPED THE REST OF HIS BOOKS IN SURPRISE, swooping up *Rip Van Winkle* from its precarious position on the edge of the boat. He flipped through the pages in fascination. Questions flooded his mind as he recalled his journey to wake the notorious dreamer. Why had Rip's story been written at all? Was Deacon himself a character? Where had Rip gone when he'd tumbled off the cliff that fateful day? Surely, he had been swept away to Wakefulness. Surely...

Was there more to the story? Had to be, or there wouldn't be a story at all.

"What do you have there?" the librarian asked, sensing his interest. "Ah, Washington Irving. He sometimes writes by the pseudonym Geoffrey Crayon or Jonathan Oldstyle. Quite the storyteller, Irving. Specializes in humor, imagery, and satire. One of those Americans."

"Pardon me, an *American*? What is an *American*?" Deacon of course lived in the perpetual present, so had no clue as to what an American was. In the present, America was Great Britain.

"An American is what a British colonialist will be Tomorrow. The Americans dream like no other. They dream as though night were eternal. I expect you will soon find evidence here in your present of the American dream of Tomorrow. It is the wildest of dreams."

Deacon found the description of the American dream concernedly similar to Rip's. He was naturally horrified at the idea of an emerging civilization of Rip Van Winkles. Such dreamers would likely plunge the province of night into a state of permanent chaos. He looked down at the unassuming book, wondering if it might foreshadow changes to come.

The librarian collected those books Deacon had dropped and placed them into a satchel. Deacon dropped *Rip Van Winkle* in along with the rest and slung the pack over his shoulder before leaping back to his own boat.

"Thank you as always, librarian. I must be off. Night is coming on, and the beacon needs turning on!"

"Shine it for me, to unpath'd waters, and undream'd shores!" the librarian responded in his best Shakespearian accent.

Deacon raced to shore. Night had arrived. Strange stars blinked to life. A fluffy, cotton-candy moon rose from the sea. The first dreamers appeared on the horizon, caught in oblivious currents, floating slowly toward the lighthouse, mesmerized by its otherworldly light — a light which needed tending.

Once ashore, Deacon proceeded to his little library, where he filed the new books. He kept with him only one title for the watch that night. After he had finished in the library, he made his way to the kitchen for a cold fish dinner and hot black tea. Black tea was a critical step in the nightly watch ritual, being just as important to beacon function as the fuel used to light it.

Deacon raced up the lighthouse stairs, cup of tea in one hand, book in the other. He hastily tended the light, replenishing the oil reservoir, trimming the wick, and igniting the transcendent flame. There was little to see in the sea. There were no dreamers in distress or dangerous conditions. The wind wasn't making speeches. It was whispering secrets, and just strong enough to turn the page of a book, making it the ideal night for reading.

Deacon sat back in the lookout chair atop the lighthouse and began his watch. Truth be told, he watched very little of the water that night. Instead, he read and re-read that peculiar account of one indelible dreamer by the name of Rip Van Winkle.

Whoever has made a voyage up the Hudson must remember the Kaatskill mountains. They are a dismembered branch of the great Appalachian family, and are seen away to the west of the river, swelling up to a noble height, and lording it over the surrounding country. Every change of season, every change of weather, indeed, every hour of the day, produces some change in the magical hues and shapes of these mountains, and they are regarded by all the good wives, far and near, as perfect barometers. When the weather is fair and settled, they are clothed in blue and purple, and print their bold outlines on the clear evening sky; but sometimes, when the rest of the landscape is cloudless, they will gather a hood of grey vapours about their summits, which, in the last rays of the setting sun, will glow and light up like a crown of glory.

At the foot of these fairy mountains, the voyager may have descried the light smoke curling up from a village, whose shingle-roofs gleam among the trees, just where the blue tints of the upland melt away into the fresh green of the nearer landscape. It is a little village, of great antiquity, having been founded by some of the Dutch colonists in the early times of the province, just about the beginning of the government of the good Peter Stuyvesant (may he rest in peace!), and there were some of the houses of the original settlers standing within a few years, built of small yellow bricks brought from Holland, having latticed windows and gable fronts, surmounted with weathercocks.

In that same village and in one of these very houses (which, to tell the precise truth, was sadly time-worn and weather-beaten), there lived, many years since, while the country was yet a province of Great Britain, a simple, *good-natured fellow, of the name of Rip Van Winkle. He was a descendant of the Van Winkles who figured so gallantly in the chivalrous days of Peter Stuyvesant, and accompanied him to the siege of Fort Christina. He inherited, however, but little of the martial character of his ancestors. I have observed that he was a simple, good-natured man; he was, moreover, a kind neighbour, and an obedient, hen-pecked husband. Indeed, to the latter circumstance might be owing that meekness of spirit which gained him such universal popularity; for those men are apt to be obsequious and conciliating abroad, who are under the discipline of shrews at home. Their tempers, doubtless, are rendered pliant and malleable in the fiery furnace of domestic tribulation; and a curtain lecture is worth all the sermons in the world for teaching the virtues of patience and long-suffering. A termagant wife may, therefore, in some respects, be considered a tolerable blessing; and if so, Rip Van Winkle was thrice blessed.*

Certain it is that he was a great favourite among all the good wives of the village, who, as usual with the amiable sex, took his part in all family squabbles; and never failed, whenever they talked those matters over in their evening gossipings, to lay all the blame on Dame Van Winkle. The children of the village, too, would shout with joy whenever he approached. He assisted at their sports, made their playthings, taught them to fly kites and shoot marbles, and told them long stories of ghosts, witches, and Indians. Whenever he went dodging about the village, he was surrounded by a troop of them, hanging on his skirts, clambering on his back, and playing a thousand tricks on him with impunity; and not a dog would bark at him throughout the neighbourhood.

The great error in Rip's composition was an insuperable aversion to all kinds of profitable labour. It could not be for want of assiduity or perseverance; for he would sit on a wet rock, with a rod as long and heavy as a Tartar's lance, and fish all day without a murmur, even though he should not be encouraged by a single nibble. He would carry a fowling-piece on his shoulder for hours together, trudging through woods and swamps, and up hill and down dale, to shoot a few squirrels or wild pigeons. He would never refuse to assist a neighbour even in the roughest toil, and was a foremost man in all country frolics for husking Indian corn, or building stone fences; the women of the village, too, used to employ him to run their errands, and to do such little odd jobs as their less obliging husbands would not do for them. In a word, Rip was ready to attend to anybody's business but his own; but as to doing family duty, and keeping his farm in order, he found it impossible.

In fact, he declared it was of no use to work on his farm; it was the most pestilent little piece of ground in the whole country; everything about it went wrong, in spite of him. His fences were continually falling to pieces; his cow would either go astray, or get among the cabbages; weeds were sure to grow quicker in his fields than anywhere else; the rain always made a point of setting in just as he had some outdoor work to do; so that though his patrimonial estate had dwindled away under his management, acre by acre, until there was little more left than a mere patch of Indian corn and potatoes, yet it was the worst-conditioned farm in the neighbourhood.

His children, too, were as ragged and wild as if they belonged to nobody. His son Rip, an urchin begotten in his own likeness, promised to inherit the habits, with the old clothes, of his father. He was generally seen trooping like a colt at his mother's heels, equipped in a pair of his father's cast-off galligaskins, which he had much ado to hold up with one hand, as a fine lady does her train in bad weather.

Rip Van Winkle, however, was one of those happy mortals, of foolish, well-oiled dispositions, who take the world easy, eat white bread or brown, whichever can be got with least thought or trouble, and would rather starve on a penny than work for a pound. If left to himself, he would have whistled life away in perfect contentment; but his wife kept continually dinning in his ears about his idleness, his carelessness, and the ruin he was bringing on his family. Morning, noon, and night, her tongue was incessantly going, and everything he said or did was sure to produce a torrent of household eloquence. Rip had but one way of replying to all lectures of the kind, and that, by frequent use, had grown into a habit. He shrugged his shoulders, shook his head, cast up his eyes, but said nothing. This, however, always provoked a fresh volley from his wife; so that he was fain to draw off his forces, and take to the outside of the house—the only side which, in truth, belongs to a hen-pecked husband.

Rip's sole domestic adherent was his dog Wolf, who was as much hen-pecked as his master; for Dame Van Winkle regarded them as companions in idleness, and even looked upon Wolf with an evil eye, as the cause of his master's going so often astray. True it is, in all points of spirit befitting an honourable dog, he was as courageous an animal as ever scoured the woods—but what courage can withstand the evil-doing and all-besetting terrors of a woman's tongue? The moment Wolf entered the house his chest fell, his tail drooped to the ground or curled between his legs, he sneaked about with a gallows air, casting many a sidelong glance at Dame Van Winkle, and at the least flourish of a broomstick or ladle he would fly to the door with yelping precipitation.

Times grew worse and worse with Rip Van Winkle as years of matrimony rolled on; a tart temper never mellows with age, and a sharp tongue is the only edged tool that grows keener with constant use. For a long while he used to console himself, when driven from home, by frequenting a kind of perpetual club of the sages, philosophers and other idle personages of the village, which held its sessions on a bench before a small inn, designated by a rubicund portrait of His Majesty George the Third. Here they used to sit in the shade through a long, lazy summer's day, talking listlessly over village gossip, or telling endless, sleepy stories about nothing. But it would have been worth any statesman's money to have heard the profound discussions that sometimes took place, when by chance an old newspaper fell into their hands from some passing traveller. How solemnly they would listen to the contents, as drawled out by Derrick Van Bummel, the schoolmaster, a dapper, learned little man, who was not to be daunted by the most gigantic word in the dictionary; and how sagely they would deliberate upon public events some months after they had taken place.

The opinions of this junto were completely controlled by Nicholas Vedder, a patriarch of the village, and landlord of the inn, at the door of which he took his seat from morning till night, just moving sufficiently to avoid the sun and keep in the shade of a large tree; so that the neighbours could tell the hour by his movements as accurately as by a sun-dial. It is true he was rarely heard *to speak, but smoked his pipe incessantly. His adherents, however (for every great man has his adherents), perfectly understood him, and knew how to gather his opinions. When anything that was read or related displeased him, he was observed to smoke his pipe vehemently, and to send forth short, frequent, and angry puffs; but when pleased, he would inhale the smoke slowly and tranquilly, and emit it in light and placid clouds; and sometimes, taking the pipe from his mouth, and letting the fragrant vapour curl about his nose, would gravely nod his head in token of perfect approbation.*

From even this stronghold the unlucky Rip was at length routed by his termagant wife, who would suddenly break in upon the tranquillity of the assemblage and call the members all to naught; nor was that august personage, Nicholas Vedder himself, sacred from the daring tongue of this terrible virago, who charged him outright with encouraging her husband in habits of idleness.

Poor Rip was at last reduced almost to despair; and his only alternative, to escape from the labour of the farm and clamour of his wife, was to take gun in hand and stroll away into the woods. Here he would sometimes seat himself at the foot of a tree, and share the contents of his wallet with Wolf, with whom he sympathised as a fellow-sufferer in persecution. "Poor Wolf," he would say, "thy mistress leads thee a dog's life of it; but never mind, my lad, whilst I live thou shalt never want a friend to stand by thee!" Wolf would wag his tail, look wistfully in his master's face; and, if dogs can feel pity, I verily believe he reciprocated the sentiment with all his heart.

In a long ramble of the kind on a fine autumnal day, Rip had unconsciously scrambled to one of the highest parts of the Kaatskill Mountains. He was after his favourite sport of squirrel shooting, and the still solitudes had echoed and re-echoed with the reports of his gun. Panting and fatigued, he threw himself, late in the afternoon, on a green knoll, covered with mountain herbage, that crowned the brow of a precipice. From an opening between the trees he could overlook all the lower country for many a mile of rich woodland. He saw at a distance the lordly Hudson, far, far below him, moving on its silent but majestic course, with the reflection of a purple cloud, or the sail of a lagging bark, here and there sleeping on its glassy bosom, and at last losing itself in the blue highlands.

On the other side he looked down into a deep mountain glen, wild, lonely, and shagged, the bottom filled with fragments from the impending cliffs, and scarcely lighted by the reflected rays of the setting sun. For some time Rip lay musing on this scene; evening was gradually advancing; the mountains began to throw their long blue shadows over the valleys; he saw that it would be dark long before he could reach the village, and he heaved a heavy sigh when he thought of encountering the terrors of Dame Van Winkle.

As he was about to descend, he heard a voice from a distance, hallooing: "Rip Van Winkle! Rip Van Winkle!" He looked round, but could see nothing but a crow winging its solitary flight across the mountain. He thought his fancy must have deceived him, and turned again to descend, when he heard the same cry ring through the still evening air: "Rip Van Winkle! Rip Van Winkle!" At the same time Wolf bristled up his back, and giving a low growl, skulked to his master's side, looking fearfully down into the glen. Rip now felt a vague apprehension stealing over him; he looked anxiously in the same direction, and perceived a strange figure slowly toiling up the rocks, and bending under the weight of something he carried on his back. He was surprised to see any human being in this lonely and unfrequented place; but supposing it to be some one of the neighbourhood in need of his assistance, he hastened down to yield it.

On nearer approach he was still more surprised at the singularity of the stranger's appearance. He was a short, square-built old fellow, with thick bushy hair, and a grizzled beard. His dress was of the antique Dutch fashion: a cloth jerkin strapped round the waist—several pair of breeches, the outer one of ample volume, decorated with rows of buttons down the sides, and bunches at the knees. He bore on his shoulder a stout keg, that seemed full of liquor, and made signs for Rip to approach and assist him with the load. Though rather shy and distrustful of his new acquaintance, Rip complied with his usual alacrity; and mutually relieving one another, they clambered up a narrow gully, apparently the dry bed of a mountain torrent. As they ascended, Rip every now and then heard long, rolling peals, like distant thunder, that seemed to issue out of a deep ravine, or rather cleft, between lofty rocks, toward which their ragged path conducted. He paused for an instant, but supposing it to be the muttering of one of those transient thunder-showers which often take place in mountain heights, he proceeded. Passing through the ravine, they came to a hollow, like a small amphitheatre, surrounded by perpendicular precipices, over the brinks of which impending trees shot their branches, so that you only caught glimpses of the azure sky and the bright evening cloud. During the whole time Rip and his companion had laboured on in silence; for though the former marvelled greatly what could be the object of carrying a keg of liquor up this wild mountain, yet there was something strange and incomprehensible about the unknown, that inspired awe and checked familiarity.

On entering the amphitheatre, new objects of wonder presented themselves. On a level spot in the centre was a company of odd-looking personages playing at nine-pins. They were dressed in a quaint, outlandish fashion; some wore short doublets, others jerkins, with long knives in their belts, and most of them had enormous breeches, of similar style with that of the guide's. Their visages, too, were peculiar; one had a large beard, broad face, and small piggish eyes; the face of another seemed to consist entirely of nose, and was surmounted by a white sugar-loaf hat, set off with a little red cock's tail. They all had beards, of various shapes and colours. There was one who seemed to be the commander. He was a stout old gentleman, with a weather-beaten countenance; he wore a laced doublet, broad belt and hanger, high-crowned hat and feather, red stockings, and high-heeled shoes, with roses in them. The whole group reminded Rip of the figures in an old Flemish painting, in the parlour of Dominie Van Shaick, the village parson, and which had been brought over from Holland at the time of the settlement.

What seemed particularly odd to Rip was, that these folks were evidently amusing themselves, yet they maintained the gravest faces, the most mysterious silence, and were, withal, the most melancholy party of pleasure he had ever witnessed. Nothing interrupted the stillness of the scene but the noise of the balls, which, whenever they were rolled, echoed along the mountains like rumbling peals of thunder.

As Rip and his companion approached them, they

suddenly desisted from their play, and stared at him with such fixed, statue-like gaze, and such strange, uncouth, lack-lustre countenances, that his heart turned within him, and his knees smote together. His companion now emptied the contents of the keg into large flagons, and made signs to him to wait upon the company. He obeyed with fear and trembling; they quaffed the liquor in profound silence, and then returned to their game.

By degrees Rip's awe and apprehension subsided. He even ventured, when no eye was fixed upon him, to taste the beverage, which he found had much of the flavour of excellent Hollands. He was naturally a thirsty soul, and was soon tempted to repeat the draught. One taste provoked another; and he reiterated his visits to the flagon so often that at length his senses were overpowered, his eyes swam in his head, his head gradually declined, and he fell into a deep sleep.

~ Twenty Years Later ~

On waking, he found himself on the green knoll whence he had first seen the old man of the glen.

The words within the book ended there, but the pages did not. There were several blank ones after. It was as though the full story had yet to be written. All the words were typed, with the exception of 'Twenty Years Later'. That was handwritten, as if to make a note which would not explicitly be called out in the text itself. The last blank page of the book was signed:

~ Washington Irving, 1819

Message in a Bottle

FOR DEACON, THE BOOK WAS REVEALING IN MORE WAYS than one. Firstly, it made more sense of Rip's initial dreaming, and his hiding away in Yesterday. The intolerance of his present; his destitute farm, 'termagant' wife, and poverty caused him to flee wakeful consciousness. In his dream, the absence of any hopeful Tomorrow naturally led him to Yesterday, where Deacon last saw him. What happened *after* Yesterday was a new question the story posed.

After Yesterday, Rip Van Winkle was still dreaming.

The book claimed Rip fell asleep for twenty years. If the legend were true, and Rip slept for even a fraction of that, then he was still asleep. Hardly a full palette of those many-colored, time-carrying winds had blown through since the boy Rip had disappeared off the cliff and into the Sea of Dreams. All that time, Deacon assumed Rip had been swept away by the tides to Wakefulness. Those tides are sentient, after all. They feel a thing, and carry it where it was meant to be. Perhaps Rip was meant to be somewhere else entirely.

Strangely, the story made no mention of that mysterious girl of his dreams. Rip called her by the name of a flower, and she was the only one he noticed among all those others falling from the sky. She was the one who the boy he had been was playfully infatuated, and the man he had become was obsessed. She was one of those deep secrets, sealed away in some cavernous corner of his beaten and bruised heart, accessible only within the furthest reaches of a dream.

Deacon wasn't totally surprised at her omission from the story. The lighthouse keeper had reeled in many such secrets over the years. The unpublished pages of history are filled with scandalous affairs, untold obsessions, and secret sexual proclivities. Here was one more.

Stranger than the absence of Rosie from the story was the absence of any dream from the story. Not a single nightly vision of the slumbering subject was suggested in the tale. A paltry paragraph break was all that represented the unconscious odyssey of Rip Van Winkle:

One taste provoked another; and he reiterated his visits to the flagon so often that at length his senses were overpowered, his eyes swam in his head, his head gradually declined, and he fell into a deep sleep.

On waking, he found himself on the green knoll whence he had first seen the old man of the glen.

The story was far from complete, and left Deacon with an uneasy feeling. If Rip were still asleep, where was he, and what trouble might he be brewing? The truant dreamer posed a risk, as did the rest of this "America." If what the librarian said was true, and there was an entirely new civilization of Rip Van Winkle-esque dreamers, an existential threat to the world as Deacon knew it was on the horizon.

Although Deacon was worried by the unexpected story, there was little he could do. There was no telling where Rip was. And even if Deacon had some clue as to his whereabouts, there would be no hurrying after him. There was no immediate need. All was well. There wasn't a cloud in the sky.

Deacon decided it best to write a letter to Faerie, warning them of the tale. Faerie was that realm of magic and mystery which went by countless names: A Land Far, Far Away, Otherworld, Elfhame, Shangri-la, Eden, Fay... It was the birthplace of all mythology, where the first gods and goddesses were deified, and the first kings and queens coronated. Faerie is where the first valorous hero lived, and where his villainous counterpart died. It is where the sons of gods perish, before (sometimes) returning to life. It is where talismans are made magic. It is where the great flood ends the world, and the few survivors rebuild it. In Faerie are the originations of all folklore, fairytale, and religion ever imagined.

Rip Van Winkle was not merely a fiction. He was a fairytale — the first ever American fairytale. Deacon suspected there would be important change to come as a result of it. Such renowned mythologies often originate from a collective chaos in the unconscious, before possessing the conscious mind. They affect the zeitgeist of whole nations, making their mark on the histories of both the waking world and dreaming one.

DEACON WROTE THE LETTER TO FAERIE ON AN unlooked-for winter's day. He hadn't expected winter because the day before had been summer. Seasons change as frequently as days on the Sea of Dreams, but the skipping of a full season from one day to the next was unusual.

Deacon spent the long, chilly day painting and oiling. "Oil it if it moves, paint it if it doesn't," as the old lighthouse saying goes. High waves could strip a coat of paint in no time. A salty wind could dry out a well-oiled machine faster than that. Deacon passed lifetimes painting and oiling. His back was feeling the lifetimes on that day. The cold has a way of creaking old goat bones.

When the day was done, he was relieved at the sight of his ship captain's desk within the library. He threw a log on the fire to thaw the frosty room and took a seat. Though physically exhausted, he found himself mentally fresh. Painting and oiling takes very little serious thought. He dipped his pen in the ink-bottle and began the letter.

DEAR FAERIE,

I WRITE FROM THE LIGHTHOUSE TO INFORM YOU OF A *matter which concerns you. In our most recent shipment of literature from Tomorrow, a fairy story of a most unexpected nature came into my possession. The tale is titled Rip Van Winkle, and is named after a man who sleeps for twenty years without interruption. I know this Rip, having encountered him many winds ago. He was quite the mischievous fellow, and had then already been sleeping for far longer than is natural. I fear he sleeps still, and that his story forebodes a peril to come. That peril lies in the content of Rip's dreams. These dreams are of a new, American style. They are wild, to say the least. It is my personal belief that these dreams may mark a permanent change in the psyche of* mankind. As a result, those timeless tales and traditions born from your shores may be at risk, or at least in for some significant transformation. I cannot say how, or the manner by which these transformations will occur, but I suspect this Rip will be involved.

IT COULD BE I AM ALARMING YOU FOR NO REASON, AND there is no need for action on your part. I hope that is the case. Please find enclosed the story of Rip Van Winkle referenced herein. I trust it finds you well, wherever you are.

YOUR HUMBLE SERVANT,
    The Principal Lighthouse Keeper

DEACON PLACED THE LETTER AND BOOK TOGETHER within a large glass jar. A message in a bottle was the standard means of corresponding with Faerie, because few knew where it was. Some say it lay down a rabbit hole, or at the back of a wardrobe. Others claim it to be more easily accessible, and that there exist more magical doorways than actual ones. Whatever the case, Deacon didn't know the way. Luckily, the sea did.

Deacon left the library and walked wearily up the lighthouse stairs to the topmost platform. He hurled the jar as far as he could, which was not far at all. Luckily, the wind carried it a safe distance before it splashed into the waves, before bobbing away on the sentient current. That was that. Deacon felt better at having sent the letter, though remained uncertain of its effect.

He made his way back down to the library for a book

121

before bed. The room was no warmer, so he added more fuel to the fire before examining the bookshelf for something to read. Tired as he was, he could only tolerate something short, so looked over the poetry titles. *Rime of the Ancient Mariner* caught his eye. He'd received the poem the same day as *Rip Van Winkle* but had yet to read it.

He lay back on a leather chaise and started reading the epigraph.

I READILY BELIEVE THAT THERE ARE MORE INVISIBLE THAN visible Natures in the universe. But who will explain for us the family of all these beings, and the ranks and relations and distinguishing features and functions of each? What do they do? What places do they inhabit? The human mind has always sought the knowledge of these things, but never attained it. Meanwhile I do not deny that it is helpful sometimes to contemplate in the mind, as on a tablet, the image of a greater and better world, lest the intellect, habituated to the petty things of daily life, narrow itself and sink wholly into trivial thoughts. But at the same time we must be watchful for the truth and keep a sense of proportion, so that we may distinguish the certain from the uncertain, day from night.

"THERE ARE MORE INVISIBLE THAN VISIBLE NATURES in the universe," echoed in the faun's tired head. He lay it back on the sofa and closed his eyes. His last thoughts before falling into a deep, dreamless sleep were of Rip. Surely, Rip was one of those unexplained, invisible natures. Perhaps he was a force of nature, destined to return with some new storm at his command.

"What book is that in your hands?" said I to my son Richard a few nights ago in a dream.

"It is the history of the United States," said he. "Shall I read a page of it to you?" "No, no," said I. "I believe in the truth of no history but in that which is contained in the Old and New Testaments." "But, sir," said my son, "this page relates to your friend Mr. Adams." "Let me see it then," said I. I read it with great pleasure and herewith send you a copy of it.

"1809. Among the most extraordinary events of this year was the renewal of the friendship and intercourse between Mr. John Adams and Mr. Jefferson, the two ex-Presidents of the United States. They met for the first time in the Congress of 1775. Their principles of liberty, their ardent attachment to their country... being exactly the same, they were strongly attracted to each other and became personal as well as political friends... A difference of opinion upon the objects and issue of the French Revolution separated them during the years in which that great event interested and divided the American people. In 1809, Mr. Adams addressed a short letter to his friend Mr. Jefferson in which he congratulated him upon his escape to the shades of retirement and domestic happiness, and concluded it with assurances of his regard and good wishes for his welfare. This letter did great honor to Mr. Adams. It discovered a magnanimity known only to great minds. Mr. Jefferson replied to this letter and reciprocated expressions of regard and esteem. These letters were followed by a correspondence of several years in which they mutually reviewed the scenes of business in which they had been engaged, and candidly acknowledged to each other all the errors of opinion and conduct into *which they had fallen during the time they filled the same station in the service of their country. Many precious aphorisms, the result of observation, experience, and profound reflection, it is said, are contained in these letters. It is to be hoped the world will be favored with a sight of them... These gentlemen sunk into the grave nearly at the same time, full of years and rich in the gratitude and praises of their country."*

~ *A dream of Benjamin Rush, signer of the Declaration of Independence, 1809. The dream prophesized both the renewal of friendship between Thomas Jefferson and John Adams, as well as the fact both would die at the same time, on the same day, July 4th, 1826, the fiftieth anniversary of the Declaration of Independence*

A Midsummer Night's Dream

THE NIGHTS PASSED WITH NO ACKNOWLEDGEMENT OF the letter from Faerie.

Busy as Deacon was, the thought of Rip Van Winkle soon fell from his mind. The lighthouse kept his body busy. The books kept his brain busy. Those subtle winds of time changed the faun. The moonlight dyed his fur silver. The sunlight burnt his skin gold. The salty sea air wrinkled his face. A lifetime of thoughts wrinkled his mind.

One fateful night, the memory of Rip returned to Deacon in the most unexpected manner. He sat atop his lighthouse on a spectacular lookout. The lookout was spectacular because it was midsummer. Midsummer night's dreams are the most unimaginable amalgamations of drama, comedy, and romance. The dawn of summer inspires a hopeful sort of havoc. It was a night of theatre for Deacon, and he had the perfect seat atop his lighthouse.

The sea was especially tumultuous that night. It served as one of the few places of total freedom for the many subjugated sleepers of the age. In the waters, free from Georgian-era norms and tradition, dreamers were transformed into their true, romantic selves. They were water sprites, sea serpents, and sailors. They were mermaids, long suffocated on dry land, set free in the dead of night, drunker on water than was possible on wine. They were wild animals, without a Yesterday or Tomorrow, without a single regret or worry for one of the few times in their lives. Splashes and waves transformed into the tentacles of some monstrous kraken, breaking harmlessly on the bare shoulders of skinny dippers, who danced and sang like sirens. *Skinny dippers!* To be seen topless in those days was a scandal, if not utter madness. There in the sea they were all mad with possibility, and passion. All Deacon could hear from the top of his lighthouse were breakers and laughter. The occasional lightning flash rent the sky from top to bottom, unleashing electrical demons throughout the air, who joined in the mayhem. The lightning was of no concern to the dreamers, because they were anything they wanted to be. Among other things, they were invincible.

Deacon puffed from a long churchwarden pipe he'd whittled himself as he watched the chaos unfold below. The chaos was of the usual, good-natured sort, so there was no need for him to do much of anything. The beacon did the real work, shining a brilliant blonde through the black. It was a fine night, one so clear that Deacon could see the indigo breeze blowing steadily to Oblivion, where the woods undoubtedly swarmed with the same pandemonium.

Later that night, after the wind had reversed its course to Wakefulness, thus clearing the sea of dreamers, Deacon observed a lone canoe drifting toward his island. In the canoe was an Indian. The sight of the Indian was not surprising. Indian cultures take dreams seriously. Many tribes believe the dream world to be as real as the physical one. They also believe that what happens in the dream world has real world consequences. The obligation of an Indian was to listen and learn from dreams, integrating those messages into daily life. For those reasons, Indians were some of the most lucid and friendly of dreamers.

Deacon watched with interest as the canoe arrived near the shore closest to the lighthouse. He quickly snuffed out his pipe and hurried down the stairs to welcome the Indian. Deacon was glad to have visitors, especially Indians because of their sincere disposition and interest in all things dreamful. He had passed many nightly watches over a peace pipe with a wise chief or curious squaw, talking over those many mysteries of the mind.

Deacon opened the lighthouse front door and greeted the Indian with a wave. The Indian greeted him back with an arrow. He shot it with such force it stuck in the lighthouse mortar behind Deacon. The frightened faun stumbled backwards, falling over his front step into the lighthouse. He rose and slammed the front door, quickly locking it before backing away. A second arrow pierced the door. Then a third. Then came the war cry.

Deacon raced up the lighthouse stairs, thoughts racing faster through his flustered mind. He wondered who the Indian was, and what he was after. Lighthouse piracy was unheard of. What riches or ransom was there to plunder from a lighthouse? Surely there was no vendetta or other personal grievance. Deacon had always been nothing but welcoming to Indians.

The Indian broke the door down just as Deacon reached the top of the lighthouse stairs. He looked down at the Indian, who happened to be looking up at the same time. The only item of clothing the warrior wore was an oversized capotain pilgrim's hat. His naked body was painted a thick, darkly colored war paint meant to terrify his enemies. It had the intended effect on Deacon. He scrambled up the ladder to the topmost platform.

Deacon looked frantically around for something to defend himself with. There wasn't much. Book. Can of oil. Matches. Paintbrush. Another book. He decided the broom was his best option. He held the pitiful staff to his chest as he waited for his foe.

He wouldn't have to wait long. The sound of the Indian's footsteps on the lighthouse stairs sounded closer and closer, until he popped his barbarous face from the platform manhole. He was a truly terrifying sight: tall, sinewy, and fully nude, with the exception of the ridiculous hat. He was drenched in red and black war paint, which made him look like a bloody, charred brave fresh from battle. The Indian's bloodshot eyes stared crazily at Deacon. Deacon's own bloodshot eyes stared warily at the tomahawk in the Indian's hand.

The lighthouse keeper struck first, with a teacup. The bit of porcelain bounced harmlessly off the Indian's chest before shattering on the ground. It had no effect but to make the Indian whoop loudly. Then he charged at Deacon, swinging the tomahawk with a wide, sweeping stroke. Deacon ducked it and struck his foe behind the kneecaps with his broom as he went hurtling by. The Indian actually fell.

Deacon was too surprised to capitalize on the blow. The Indian rose and felt the back of his knee. The strike had done no serious damage. The Indian turned around, laughing a deep and maniacal laugh. He charged again, this time holding the tomahawk high above his head. Deacon tried the same duck-and-slash maneuver but tripped over his own hooves. He lay defenseless. The Indian stopped just short of his prey, raising his weapon for the death blow.

Deacon had resigned himself to his fate, when it changed. A literal knight in shining armor appeared as if from nowhere behind the Indian. He wore a silver pigface bascinet and breastplate upon which a red lion insignia was branded. In his hand was an immense, basket-hilted broadsword. Deacon had no idea who he was, or why he was there.

The Indian turned to face the newly arrived guest just in time to see the broadsword plunge through his chest. The warrior wore a look of wonder before combusting into a mist of moonbeams. Hazy remnants of warpaint drifted up into the night sky, before blowing off in the direction of Wakefulness. In moments, the Indian (wherever he was) would be startled awake by the nightmarish encounter with the knight.

Deacon rose from the lighthouse platform in amazement. He had not seen a knight in ages.

"Good evening," was all he could think to say.

"A fine evening." The knight removed his gauntlet and extended his hand.

"Who might you be?" Deacon asked as he extended his own sweaty hand.

"I am the last knight. You, I presume, are the last lighthouse keeper?"

Deacon invited the knight for a proper introduction and refreshment in his quarters. It was the least he could do. He also sought an explanation for his near-death experience at the hands of the Indian, as well as the knight's valiant intervention.

"My sincerest thanks for your help. I have never seen a

savage so, so... so savage..." Deacon muttered over a tall glass of his strongest spirit. "To what do I owe your fortuitous arrival?"

"We received your message in a bottle." The knight laid a letter on the table. Deacon recognized it as the same one he had thrust into the sea long ago. "It was a mistake not to take it seriously when we first received it. There is a danger to Faerie, as you had foretold. I had not expected that danger to arrive here already, but clearly it has."

It had been so long since Deacon penned the letter, its contents (and Rip) were nearly forgotten. In the months following his writing it, he kept a sharp watch for any peculiarities on the sea, but there were none. The nights passed, and with them the worry that Rip Van Winkle was out there somewhere, deeply sleeping, dreaming.

"What might an Indian have to do with Rip Van Winkle?" Deacon wondered. "Did Rip send him here to scalp me?"

"Not exactly," the knight explained as he removed his armor. "The Indian is likely one of a growing number of dreamers in rebellion."

"Rebellion? Against what, exactly?"

"Everything — all that you, I, and the sea itself are made of. All the symbols, songs, and stories used to make sense of the world. All the lore and legends used to form the very idea of reality. Right and wrong. Good versus evil. Morals. Divinity. Sovereignty. Sanity..."

"All of those belief systems originating in Faerie," Deacon pointed out.

"Faerie itself," the knight whispered, "and with it, the fabric of this dominion of dreams, which as you know is entwined with all those ideas birthed from Faerie since the dawn of time. The destruction of those means the destruction of everything, including this very lighthouse, and the endless sea it serves."

Deacon looked out the window. The first morning light was settling the wild night. The sea was calm as ever. There wasn't a dreamer in sight. The idea of a cataclysm seemed impossible.

"I've seen no evidence of an insurrection in these parts," Deacon pointed out.

"What do you make of the Indian? Have you ever seen a man so possessed? He was one of thousands under the influence of an idea, and a leader, intending to overthrow the world as we know it, starting with Faerie."

"Is Faerie under siege?"

"Not yet, but these belligerent fantasists swarm our seas. They rise like drowned phantasms from the depths without warning. They sink our ships, impress our sailors, and harass our trading outposts. We think it will not be long before there is an organized assault."

"And who would be so bold as to organize such an assault?"

"Rip Van Winkle. We have reason to believe he is their general. As you stated in your letter, he represents a change in the age and temperament of mankind. A new fashion of dream..."

"An American dream," Deacon finished for the knight. "Of what aid can a lowly lighthouse keeper provide? I suppose that is why you have come here, to ask for my help?"

"I was dispatched here by the king of kings himself. I am to bring you to Faerie where you will stand before the royal court as soon as can be. We ask only for your counsel in the handling of these affairs, and of the nature of this everlasting dreamer, Rip Van Winkle."

Deacon finished his drink and poured another. He wanted no part in a journey to Faerie, or any other destination involving Rip Van Winkle. The memory of all those misadventures in the overlong quest to awaken Rip came back to mind. But there was also the situation to consider. He had very nearly been tomahawked to death in his own lighthouse.

"I should like the night to think the matter over," Deacon concluded.

The faun showed the knight to the guest bedroom before making his own way to bed. He tossed and turned for what seemed like forever, restless as ever. Thoughts of Rip, Faerie, and the Indian cycled endlessly through his tired head. Unable to sleep, he stopped trying. He rose, and with his little oil lantern made his way to the library. A book would settle him down.

He selected *The Odyssey*, one of those reliable tales that never let him down. He climbed wearily to the top of the lighthouse for another read. He may as well enjoy the view while he still had it.

Odysseus was a prolific dreamer. Many of his renowned wanderings took place in the Sea of Dreams. Deacon had observed him once from on high, his galley tossing and turning in the tidal clutches of Poseidon. Some of the isles he visited were nearby. The land of the lotus-eaters was a tramp toward morning. Calypso, the possessive nymph who detained Odysseus for seven years, lived just a stone's throw from the Sleeping Siren. Deacon saw her there on occasion, always in some unapproachable corner, sipping only the finest of Eleusinian Mysteries.

Deacon skipped to the end of the book, wondering if there was any indication as to where Odysseus traveled to after finally returning home. Faerie, surely. All fabled figures find their way to that epicenter of epics. What would they think of a lighthouse keeper in such a place? Could the faun pass for anything useful? A hero, perhaps? The wizard had suggested as much.

The words consumed those last bits of worry which kept him awake, as words have a tendency to do. He put the book down and looked out across the sea for what he supposed to be one of the last times. He wondered how it would look without the beacon. *Dark*. Too dark to dream. Deacon slogged down the lighthouse stairs to his bedroom, where he collapsed into such a darkness.

THE SUN WAS HIGH AND HAUGHTY WHEN DEACON ROSE. He looked out his bedroom window at the gleaming sea. The knight was at the dock preparing his ship for the voyage to Faerie. Without his armor he could pass for a sailor. The sea spray dried his long blonde hair into tangled straw. His skin was that sun-roasted, sandy shade. His forearms were knotted with muscle for rope work. He had the grit needed to withstand the long, lonely days at sea.

Deacon hurriedly prepared the tried-and-true combination of cockles and mussels for breakfast. He couldn't bare leaving without feasting on his store of cockles and mussels, hard to gather as they were back in those days. He and the knight ate at the kitchen table nearest the window facing Oblivion. Deacon looked out as he ate, guessing it to be the general direction of Faerie.

"Tell me knight, in what direction is Faerie?"

"Ask not the direction, but the road. The way to Faerie winds like a slithering serpent. The road there is different from others. Being far more dangerous, it is far less traveled.

133

Maps cannot mark it. Men cannot pave it. It twists and turns crazily, making it easy to stray from. It is the only road with an end truly worthy of reaching. And few have..."

"Is there a name for such a road?"

"It goes by many names; the path less trodden, the road not taken, the way less travelled..."

"Where does it begin?"

"Its origins are different for each of us. For one like you, who has passed all his days in this faraway lighthouse, all we must do is lose sight of the shore. Out on the open sea, we will happen upon the road not taken in no time at all, for it will be all around us."

They set forth that afternoon, headed nearer to Yesterday than Oblivion. It was a fine day for sailing. The sky above was as blue as the sea below. The winds were a bumblebee yellow and comfortably strong. Their ship was a nimble vessel, sliding up and down the waves as naturally as if it were a creature of the sea.

They had just lost sight of the lighthouse when the waves grew higher. Then higher still. The sea was soon transformed into what looked like a moving mountain range. The knight navigated the precipitous waves with ease, scaling each peak and descending the opposite side, before climbing another. When it seemed the waves could get no higher, they made one last climb.

Just as they reached the peak, the ship took flight. It went soaring higher and higher over the sea, straight toward the sun. The take-off was so unexpected, and the angle of flight so extreme, Deacon nearly fell overboard in those first moments. He clutched at the mast for dear life until the knight leveled the ship.

"A word of warning prior to take-off would be kindly received next time, sir knight."

"My apologies." The knight turned from the wheel. "Do relax. We will soon be in calmer seas."

Deacon found it difficult to take the advice. How would they soon be in calmer seas, flying higher and higher above rough ones? Even more disturbing was the fact the ship's sails had caught those swift, high altitude jet streams. They were soaring up and away at a tremendous speed, headed directly for the belly of a bloated, beastly-shaped cloud. It was all Deacon could do not to scream as they entered it just above the navel.

The innards of the cloud began as a fine mist, but the further they sailed through, the thicker the moisture became. Soon, it was as though they were traveling through a waterfall. Deacon was thoroughly soaked. It seemed as though the whole ship would soon be completely underwater. Just when Deacon felt about to drown, the ship burst forth from the cloud-turned-water, splashing onto the surface of a brand-new sea, beneath another sunny sky.

Deacon wiped his eyes clean of cloud, shocked at what he saw. The new waters were not only calm but crystal clear, much different from the impenetrable depths he was accustomed to. It was obvious they were in some new and distant sea.

Looking up from the water to the horizon for which they sailed, Deacon beheld Faerie for the first time. It was a kingdom of crystal, glinting in the sun as if consumed with white flames. It shone a light mightier than a thousand lighthouse beacons. The dripping-wet faun stood stupefied by the majesty of that secret city thriving on the sea above the sea.

"Behold, the forefather of all royal dominions, realms, and empires. Here is where every nation state and its mythos were spawned," the knight declared. "Is it as you imagined?"

"Such places are beyond imagination," muttered Deacon.

"I hope not beyond saving," responded the knight.

It is true that Dream is not unconnected with Faerie. In dreams strange powers of the mind may be unlocked. In some of them a man may for a space wield the power of Faerie, that power which, even as it conceives the story, causes it to take living form and colour before the eyes. A real dream may indeed sometimes be a fairy-story of almost elvish ease and skill— while it is being dreamed. But if a waking writer tells you that his tale is only a thing imagined in his sleep, he cheats deliberately the primal desire at the heart of Faerie: the realization, independent of the conceiving mind, of imagined wonder. It is often reported of fairies (truly or lyingly, I do not know) that they are workers of illusion, that they are cheaters of men by "fantasy"; but that is quite another matter. That is their affair. Such trickeries happen, at any rate, inside tales in which the fairies are not themselves illusions; behind the fantasy real wills and powers exist, independent of the minds and purposes of men.

~ *J.R.R. Tolkien, On Fairy Stories, 1939*

Faerie

SOME KINGDOMS ARE MADE FOR WAR, WITH ARROW slits for windows carved among towering stone ramparts. Others are made for revelry, surrounded with hills of barley for malting and drinking within great dining halls. Many kingdoms are barren, dotted throughout with moss-covered tombstones and the roaming ghosts of dead kings and queens. Mythical kingdoms sit on clouds in the sky, and are accessible only through stories like this, by those who still believe stories like this. Faerie was the first of those mythical kingdoms.

Deacon and the knight sailed through a series of chain gates within rows of high seawalls which acted as a layered defensive mechanism. There was little sea traffic, so they sailed quickly onward. Tall guards holding taller pikes looked down upon the faun with curiosity. Many greeted the knight with a wave and welcome. The two were expected.

Deacon had been eagerly anticipating their docking within the city once they had sailed beyond the outer walls, but no such thing occurred. They sailed on because they had to, because the roads were waterways. The kingdom was crisscrossed with a vast, complicated network of canals. The sea level inexplicably rose as they made their way toward the center of the city where the royal castle towered above everything. Deacon could see the sky-scraping keep rise in the distance, and the waterways flowing upward toward it in defiance of gravity.

They sailed slowly up the crowded canals. The kingdom was bustling with every class of citizen, from every walk of life. There were dark elves, light elves, goblins, hobgoblins, wood trolls, river trolls, mountain dwarves, hill dwarves, drunk dwarves, girls, guys, and golems. They sold goods within crowded markets, labored on the construction of homes and bridges, and when the day was done, dined and drank within waterfront taverns and terraces. It was as functioning and civilized as any dominion of dreams, or reality.

For the lighthouse keeper the sights of the city were captivating, but often overwhelming. He had been isolated on his remote island for so long, his senses were wholly unprepared. Because all things are relative, to Deacon the city seemed vaster than was possible for any city dweller to comprehend. Only a lighthouse keeper knows that astonished feeling of re-entering society after a long and lonely tour of duty. The onslaught of color, sound, and motion left him paralyzed at times.

They cruised up and along the river-road until they were before the castle walls. The canal narrowed as it traveled below the archway of a small gatehouse. The guards raised the portcullis and they sailed underneath the archway where their voyage ended in a great, glowing courtyard.

There were perfectly trimmed hedges lining golden

glass walkways. An enormous fountain of pink ruby rose from the garden. There was every color flower, everywhere. A handful of stone gargoyles perched about. No one else was to be seen.

The knight led Deacon through the courtyard to the castle keep. The keep looked like one of those supremely secret and strange medieval cathedrals. The stone edges were curved but distorted in some places. The color of the stone was swirled and smeared in certain spots, like a Van Gogh painting come to life. Two tall arched doors of a gleaming wood with golden strap hinges made Deacon think there was something important inside, something unexpected. There was.

The keep was majestically furnished. There were coats of arms, suits of armor, red carpets, magic carpets, tapestries, fireplaces on fire, tapestries of fireplaces on fire, and people. Lots of people. There were courtiers, cooks, falconers, cellarers, chanceries, knights, even the odd ghost. The great hall was so greatly busy no one took notice of the two as they walked in. No one that is, except for the king and queen, who sat at the far end of the great hall.

The queen sat on a throne. The king sat on his hind legs, because he was a lion. They were surrounded by dozens of princes and princesses — all children. Children are the noble inheritors of imagination, the last bastion of a dreamful way of life.

Deacon followed the knight nervously down the long hall, wondering what the proper etiquette was when introducing yourself to royalty. Should he bow? Kneel? What would they say? What would he say? Was he to be knighted? Was he to be eaten? Does the diet of a lion include faun?

Deacon followed the knight's lead and knelt before the

dais. The many princes and princesses took notice and began circling around. The hall fell silent.

"You may rise," the king commanded. "Welcome to Faerie, master lighthouse keeper. I hope you found your way here without harm? Even our once sacred seas are no longer safe."

The lion looked and sounded like everything a king once symbolized: decency, courage, and wisdom. It was no coincidence the creature was the emblem of countless ruling dynasties. Deacon stared in stunned silence, mesmerized by the imperial eminence of the animal.

"Your Majesty, I came upon the principal lighthouse keeper in grave danger," the knight recounted. "I slew a lone warrior atop the lighthouse itself."

The court gave a collective gasp.

"A sign of the storm to come," the queen pointed out. "One warrior forebodes many. If the lighthouse is already under siege, it will not be long before Faerie is as well."

"What do you know of my lighthouse?" Deacon found the courage to ask. The queen spoke as though the lighthouse were a royal possession.

"We see the lonely forever candle you light in your ivory tower. You shine that beacon upon the sea and spread its light in your own way. But that light also spreads here, for this place is the looking glass which reflects it. Faerie receives and returns the light, transforming all those visions of the night into the symbols and stories we use to make sense of the world."

"*STORIES!*" the king roared in command.

A courtier approached on cue, placing a small book into Deacon's hands.

Steve Wiley

Rip Van Winkle

"We understand you read stories, lighthouse keeper." The queen's voice sounded faint after the king's roar. "Did you enjoy this one?"

"Aye, Your Highness. That one is a most tangled yarn. It is like nothing else I have read, or lived."

"I have read stories like this one, tales of never-ending slumbers," the queen explained. "Epimenides is said to have fallen asleep for fifty-seven years in a cave sacred to Zeus. The Seven Sleepers of Ephesus supposedly slept in a cave for some two hundred years to escape the Roman persecution of Christians. German folktales tell of a goatherd named Peter Klaus who tasted an enchanted wine and fell asleep for twenty years—"

"—Stories without merit," interrupted the king. "Rip Van Winkle is a story with substance, history. Tell us lighthouse keeper, what do you know of this man?"

"I first learned of his errant dreaming long ago, when it brewed up a seemingly deathless storm. I set out to find and wake him, to settle the sea. I journeyed far from home, under strange stars and to stranger shores, before finally finding him. He was well in the past. He was only a boy when I came upon him in the woods, but a clever one. Before I could wake him, he disappeared with a wish into the sea. I had not heard of him again until I received this book."

"What does he seek?" the queen asked. "Power, riches, glory?"

"Rip is no ordinary man. I believe he seeks not glory, but obscurity. Not power, but the annihilation of it. Riches he strives for, but not those counted in coins. Time is his preferred currency—"

"—Time, the ultimate measure of freedom," the queen interrupted. "Here he has a limitless supply."

"There is also the matter of a girl," Deacon added.

"There is always the matter of girl," the lion agreed.

"He called her Rosie. They were together when I first found Rip. Children they were, playing at games, and well in love. When he slipped away into the sea, she leapt after him. Interestingly, there is not a single mention of Rosie in the book."

"Lost loves are by their very nature unrecorded," the queen declared. "It comes as no surprise to me that there is no mention of her in the story. She was a secret, cunningly hidden within that hinterland of dormant memories."

"Where we dream, such hidden secrets may be found and revealed," the king pronounced.

———

DEACON REMAINED IN CONVERSATION WITH THE KING and queen for a long time. They continued in their discussion of Rip, and the trouble recently faced throughout the kingdom by the growing number of piratical dreamers under his sway. The mood in the court was forlorn. It became increasingly obvious to Deacon that there was an expectation of an assault on Faerie and that there was little to be done to prevent or defend it.

When the conversation ended, Deacon was led through one of the many adjoining corridors to a staircase that led up to his room. His room was a large one of silver stone, the walls blushing from the glow of a small fireplace. A map of the dreamland hung above the fireplace, marking his position within the heavens. An immense canopy bed occupied the center of the room. There was one window on the wall behind the bed that held a view of the kingdom below.

Deacon fell asleep the instant his horns hit the pillow. He was exhausted from the voyage to Faerie and the polite but extensive interrogation administered by the king and queen. He lay asleep a long time, happily oblivious of Rip, Faerie, and the uncertain hereafter.

In the dead of night, a curiously strong wind entered the room through the window, flapping the canopy curtains wildly about. The faun stumbled out of bed. He found himself drawn to the source of the wind, and the window. He sought not to close it, but to look outside it.

Deacon's chamber was set atop one of the tallest towers of the castle. Looking out the window, his tired eyes travelled over the silent city, beyond it to the great seawalls, then further still, to the infinite expanse of dark dream sea dotted here and there with whitecaps like stray sailboats adrift in the night. Then, something closer captured his attention.

It was just below his room on the castle ramparts where the guards kept watch, only this was no guard. It was a woman in a flowing white dress. The dress was blowing so uncontrollably in the wind, Deacon thought she might blow away altogether. She stood there unmoving, looking up to him in the window, facing him with an inviting stare. Deacon was tired, and in no mood for a midnight tryst, yet something drew him to the woman. Even from afar, he sensed something vaguely familiar about her.

Deacon quickly dressed and lit a candle from the dying fireplace to light his way. He quietly slipped out of his chamber, proceeding down the stairs and through a door which he correctly guessed led to the castle walls. Walking outside, he found the woman still standing there on the ramparts, looking out over the city toward the sea, as if waiting for something, or someone. Deacon shuffled slowly toward her.

"A fine night," was all Deacon could think to say.

"Is it?" The woman turned to look at him. "The wind is bitter."

She cast no shadow in the moonlight. Her silver hair wafted like smoke in the wind. He had seen those wandering, wild eyes before, their robin egg blue color unmistakable. They were the eyes of a dreamer, of a grown-up Rosie O'Ryan. Soon she would be awake, and the faun would be a figment of forgotten night.

"What is your name?" she asked.

"Why, I am merely a dream. Whoever named a dream?"

"I should think a dream's name is important. It would help me to remember you when I awaken."

"If you remembered me at all when you woke, you would only remember my type; hero, villain, monster, man..."

"Well then, what *type* are you?"

Deacon wasn't entirely sure. Was he a lighthouse keeper? Was that a type? He looked out over the kingdom toward the sea beyond for some ray of guidance from the beacon that was his life's work. There was no sign of it. Perhaps it had already been forever snuffed out.

"I am an everyman," Deacon muttered. "Less a reason to remember me."

"I will remember you," she assured him.

"I doubt that, but thank you."

"You're welcome. Where exactly are we, if you don't mind my asking?"

"Didn't you know? We are in the heart of Faerie."

"I thought so. I once dreamt of this realm when I was a girl. It has been so long since I've visited, I'd almost forgotten it entirely. I remember it now. I recall waiting on these walls for some prince to find and rescue me. I must still be waiting for him after all these years."

"You are waiting for Rip Van Winkle, I presume?" Deacon guessed at the prince's identity.

"How did you know?" She turned to him, less visible by the second.

Deacon looked out over the castle walls. The kingdom was still and silent, except for the faintest of echoes from the distant sea. Gazing that way, Deacon saw the thinnest layer of velvet illuminate the far horizon. The light revealed a sea dotted with ominous black sails. The dark armada was ominous not because it was there, but because it was dawn. Nightmares occur just before the dawn.

"It seems your prince has arrived at last," Deacon said to Rosie.

But she was gone with the night.

For this and all other changes in my dreams were accompanied by deep-seated anxiety and gloomy melancholy, such as are wholly incommunicable by words. I seemed every night to descend, not metaphorically, but literally to descend, into chasms and sunless abysses, depths below depths, from which it seemed hopeless that I could ever reascend. Nor did I, by waking, feel that I had reascended. This I do not dwell upon; because the state of gloom which attended these gorgeous spectacles, amounting at last to utter darkness, as of some suicidal despondency, cannot be approached by words.

~ *A nightmare of Thomas De Quincey, from* Confessions of an English Opium-Eater, *1821*

The Nightmare

In any book of dreams there must of course be a nightmare. This being an uncommon dream, it was darkened with an uncommon nightmare. The nightmare was not to be helplessly slept through, nor was it to be rescued from upon waking. The nightmare did not begin with a vision of ghastly spirits, grotesque monsters, or death itself. It began with a fairy.

The last knight woke in his chamber to the fairy sitting cross-legged on his dresser. You may think that a pleasant sight to wake to, but it was not. It was terrifying. Fairies in those days were not the playful Tinkerbells and well-meaning godmothers of later stories. The word fairy stems from the Latin word *fata*, which means "fate." They were omens of catastrophe.

The knight had expected an attack on the kingdom any day. The moment he saw the fairy, he knew that day had come. The fairy itself was not a thing to be frightened of. It sat there quietly observing him, wings folded protectively over her body like the statue of some fallen angel.

The thing to be truly frightened of was the secret the

fairy kept — the spell, enchantment, or other mischievous magic. Fairies are tricksters. The trickster is cunning and dangerous, gleefully defying the laws of man to change the course of his history, or maybe just to play.

The knight rose from bed and walked to the fairy. Her wings lifted in interest, a puckish smile on her face. He reached his hand out to touch her. Just before he was able to lay a finger on her, she leapt into the air and darted out the bedroom window.

Moments after she'd flown away the belfry rang a warning to the kingdom, signaling all men-at-arms to the battlements. The knight was unsurprised. He prepared himself for what he believed to be his final contest. He donned his finest suit of armor. He cleaned and sheathed his sword. He left his shield behind, knowing all too well there was no defense from destiny.

———

THE KNIGHT SOON FOUND HIMSELF ATOP THE OUTER-most seawalls. Those walls were the tallest and thickest, being the first line of defense. The sky was dim, but the sea shone bright from the fires burning here and there within the enemy fleet. The sea was so crowded with the black-sailed ships, one could walk from boat to boat for miles in any direction.

The siege began all at once. Thousands of ladders fell upon the kingdom walls with uncanny synchronicity. Legions of demon-haunted dreamers speedily scaled them, trampling over the defenders in a demented fury.

The knight watched in disbelief as his compatriots were hurled from the walls like mangled marionettes. Troops of phantoms overcame those who remained. Whole sections of the seawall collapsed under the weight of the dark army. Enemy ships streamed through the gaps like a ceaseless black ink staining the once clear sea.

The knight fought bravely on the walls alongside many others, but their defense was futile. They were outnumbered and overpowered. Like debilitated dreamers in the midst of a nightmare, their strikes were weakened. The knight felt heavy, as though he wore a dozen or more suits of armor. He swung his sword in slow, powerless strokes, occasionally landing a blow on some unlucky foe, but mostly missing or falling harmlessly aside.

The sun rose with a remarkable flash, momentarily blinding the knight and few others who remained with him on the hopelessly overrun walls. As he shielded his eyes, he was struck in the breastplate. The force of the blow sent him tumbling down the stairs leading up to the ramparts. The flustered knight rose, continuing down the stairs to the dock below.

There, he boarded a boat rescuing the few remaining defenders. They sailed toward the city in organized retreat, the sky darkening once again. The sun sank back over the horizon from whence it came, as though it had beheld the day to come, and decided against it. A few solitary stars kept their lonely watch above, twirling and blinking in astonishment.

Looking up at the reinstated night sky, the knight noticed what he thought to be two newly arrived stars behaving unnaturally. The stars danced awkwardly in the darkness, like a pair of faraway fireflies. Then they grew larger, and climbed higher, as if they were the headlights of some soaring ghost train.

Attacker and defender alike stopped fighting and stared in silent wonder at the mysterious, now fast approaching lights. The wind strengthened as they drew near. The knight watched until they were upon the kingdom, until it became clear what it was they were. When he discerned the simmering source, his curiosity turned to dread — they were the smoldering eyes of a vast, gold and garnet dragon.

The knight watched in horror as the dragon swooped down, hovering low over a seawall. The serpent inhaled with such might, it seemed to suck all the oxygen from the air itself. The knight struggled to catch his breath, choking in despair as the dragon vomited a stream of white-hot flame, incinerating all those on the battlements.

The knight sailed through the crumbling, scorched seawalls toward the city, with seemingly every ship in the sea in pursuit of him. Shadowy multitudes flooded under, over, and straight through the once impenetrable defenses. When several attacking ships were nearly upon him, the knight's boat slipped through the main city gates that were then closed behind him.

The gate closure did little to slow the siege and the city was soon overrun. Civilians fled here and there in a panicked frenzy. The dragon soared overhead, occasionally hurtling down, burning indiscriminately. In no time at all it had transformed the network of canals into a web of flames. Clever sparks leapt nimbly from roof to roof, carried through the air in the arms of the dark day's wind. Buildings became bonfires. Fires crackled and roared over the shrieks and wails of the helpless inhabitants.

The knight made his way to the castle where he intended to make his last stand. He rushed through the shambles of the once illustrious capital, now the picture of damnation. Most of the canals were blocked with collapsed, burning buildings. Those that weren't blocked looked like flowing quagmires of molten gold. Charred bodies littered the few accessible paths. It took careful navigation to find a route to the castle, through a narrow network of alleyways and bridges, on those few remaining safe roads.

When the knight did finally reach the castle gates, he was surprised to find them intact. He turned to look down over the kingdom one last time as if all might be well, and the day's events no more than a passing night terror. It was a view of utter ruin. More fires had sprouted, their sparks drifting up in search of the stars through ash and smoke. The castle somehow remained untouched. It was as though the siege were a cyclone, and the castle its undisturbed eye.

The knight found the king and queen in a still and silent throne room. They appeared to be the only two left. All the little princes and princesses of the court had disappeared. There were no guards or servants, or were there? Who was that figure hiding in the corner? It was the lighthouse-keeping faun, standing on his trembling goat-legs, looking too frightened to move. The knight nodded to him, wondering why the faun hadn't already fled.

Another shadowy figure revealed himself from the curtains behind the throne. The man was draped in an extraordinary cloak, stitched with nightmares. The nightmares moved as he moved, making it look as though he were standing in front of a film projector. There were the crumbled ruins of an ancient city on his chest, surrounded by crowds of refugees marching across his shoulders. Graves polka-dotted one arm. Whole castles collapsed down his stomach into the river which ran across his waist like a belt. Fast-ticking, grimacing clock faces lined the bottom trim of the cloak, as if to say the knight's time had come. It had.

The king and queen sat stoically on their thrones as the darkly clad guest sauntered between them toward the knight. He was a long-haired, bushy-bearded man of middle-age, with faded gray eyes. Rows of crooked, rotted teeth smiled nefariously at the knight, inviting him to fight.

The knight drew his sword in acceptance of the invitation. The man drew his own. The knight charged him with a wrath that forced his opponent out through the throne room door. There in the corridor, the two began the last duel of the last knight, which would mark the end of Faerie. It would last for all that was left of the dark day.

The combat looked like something out of a medieval-era mural depicting the Archangel Michael waging war with Satan. That is to say, it looked unnatural. The two moved together in a fatal rhythm so precise it seemed choreographed. They fought the day away in the throne room, through the castle halls, in the garden, back to the throne room, upon the castle walls, and elsewhere.

The conquerors stormed the castle, but none intervened in the sacred contest. The king was last seen on the battlements, a lion grown in his rage to supernatural proportions. Pinpricked with arrows and swords, he fought the dragon with all the stubbornness of a dying folklore. It was said when the king was finally slain, his death-roar collapsed the castle keep.

How the queen met her fate, none could say. A queen is as secretive in death as she is in life. All that is known with certainty is she vanished with the rest of the dream that was Faerie.

At the end of it all, the knight and his rival found themselves on the narrow, stone bridge which crossed the moat to the castle. Each was soaked in his own blood. The knight's was an ordinary red. The cloaked man's glowed green like the flash of first sun in the morning or the last at sunset. It stained the whole of the moat, so it could have been mistaken for a grass path.

The knight was bested on the bridge as all heroes are: not by brute force or physical mastery, but by trickery. Heracles was tricked to death with the poisoned cloak of Nessus. Osiris was deceived into the grave by his brother, Set. Sir Galahad was betrayed by a belief in the Holy Grail. The last knight was fooled by the same style trickery. His trickster was the fairy.

Just when it seemed the knight finally had the upper hand, a fairy drifted down from the castle walls. The knight recognized the fairy as the same one from his bedroom that morning. The fairy carried with her a secret, as all fairies do. She had waited until his most vulnerable moment to reveal the secret. That particular secret was a weapon without equal, one inconspicuous, yet lethal. The secret was a kiss.

The fairy was upon the knight in an instant. She snuck him the kiss with a suddenness he could not defend against. Being both a first and last kiss, it was more powerful than either. The knight was blindsided. He stood helplessly on the bridge, unable to move a single step.

The knight's cloaked adversary marched forth in triumph. The nefarious grin returned to his face as he kicked the knight squarely in the chest. The force of the blow sent the knight soaring over the side of the bridge toward the moat below.

The knight hadn't noticed his helmet was gone until he saw his hair. Blonde tresses whipped all around his face as he fell, the air rushing swiftly by. He reached for something, anything to grab hold of. He fell for what seemed like an eternity, for so long he thought he might actually be flying.

The sensation of falling is common within nightmares. Just before the dreamer hits the ground, they are supposed to wake with a startle. Dreamers are not supposed to hit the ground, just as heroes are not supposed to die. But they sometimes do.

The knight would not splash into the water, nor would he wake with a startle. Time had at last discovered the timeless kingdom. The bell tower chimed midnight. The moat transformed into a gaping chasm of darkness. The knight would disappear into that chasm after the fashion of all fairytale knights in shining armor — with one last ruinous legend, ending in one last kiss.

A change came o'er the spirit of my dream.
  The Boy was sprung to manhood: in the wilds
  Of fiery climes he made himself a home,
  And his Soul drank their sunbeams; he was girt
  With strange and dusky aspects; he was not
  Himself like what he had been; on the sea
  And on the shore he was a wanderer;
  There was a mass of many images
  Crowded like waves upon me, but he was
  A part of all; and in the last he lay
  Reposing from the noontide sultriness,
  Couched among fallen columns, in the shade
  Of ruined walls that had survived the names
  Of those who reared them; by his sleeping side
  Stood camels grazing, and some goodly steeds
  Were fastened near a fountain; and a man,
  Glad in a flowing garb, did watch the while,
  While many of his tribe slumbered around:
  And they were canopied by the blue sky,
  So cloudless, clear, and purely beautiful,
  That God alone was to be seen in heaven.

~ The Dream, by Lord Byron, 1817

Why we Dream

Deacon was one of the few to remain in the castle during the siege. He would have fled, but there was nowhere to flee. The kingdom was surrounded by an impenetrable, black-sailed armada. The faun watched helplessly from on high as the city fell. He watched as the walls crumbled into the sea, and the buildings after. He watched as the canals clogged with fire, and the conquerors stormed the castle. He watched the last of the last knight.

When the knight was slain, the stars were slain along with him. All at once they closed their silver eyes in sorrow and were outshone by the late-rising sun. The faun lay hidden in the garden as the castle was looted. It was there he was captured.

He was surprised to have been captured and not killed, though at times he wished he'd been killed. He was bound, gagged, and blindfolded before being tossed into the bottom of a rowboat. He soon found himself back at sea where he was transferred to a large galley.

When the blindfold came off, Deacon found himself in the cargo hold of the ship. As he sat chained to the wall, he

157

felt nothing like himself. He was a faun. Fauns are half-human, half-goat. Deacon had always considered himself a civilized specimen, far more human than goat. But in that hold he was all goat, and treated like one. He fed on garbage. He pissed and shat in the corner. He slept on a bed of damp, rotten hay. A goatish stench filled every inch of the prison. Deacon lay in the despondent darkness for what seemed like days.

One evening, he heard the echo of heavy footsteps coming down the ship stairs, through the passage, and toward his cell. He hadn't seen light in so long that when the hallway filled with it, he thought he was hallucinating. Whatever he was expecting, it certainly wasn't what arrived.

That darkly cloaked conqueror of the kingdom peered through the steel bars, his face glowing from the candelabra he carried. His eyes shone wide beneath big bushy eyebrows. Deacon of course recognized him from the siege, but also from somewhere else.

"I look familiar," the man guessed at Deacon's thoughts, "because we met once, long ago. I am Rip Van Winkle. Would you care to join me for dinner on the upper deck?"

DEACON EMERGED FROM THE BOWELS OF THE SHIP TO A hazy, tropical twilight. The ship was one of those brawny galleys from the Golden Age of Piracy. The wood was warped and weathered. The riggings were taut, but worn with age. Bamboo lanterns dangled from the masts like a family of fallen stars. The moon shone brightly through the mist — a gargantuan, glowing ball of coconut flesh over the cerulean sea.

Deacon made his way to a candle-lit table for two where Rip sat waiting for him. Deacon saw remnants of the boy in the man. Childish freckles drowned in the depths of his bottomless beard, but the bright, boyish eyes remained. Rip's once amber hair looked to have been dyed darker by the everlasting night, yet remained wild and free as ever.

"Welcome to my ship. Allow me to offer my sincerest apologies for your initial accommodations. Your presence below deck was made known to me only recently."

Deacon was pleasantly surprised by the apologetic tone.

"Rest assured, we will upgrade your cabin this very evening. Now please, sit down. It is dinnertime. We have much to eat, and discuss."

Deacon took a seat across from his captor-turned-host. The pair were served an extravagant dinner by a peg-legged, Long John Silver-looking deck hand turned waiter. They were brought the finest of wines and all the best of what the dream sea had to offer: escargot, caviar, oysters, lobster, and more. The conversation was as unexpectedly pleasant as the meal.

"I understand you are the principal lighthouse keeper," said Rip. "How unique a trade. Tell me, what do you enjoy most about it?"

"The parts I enjoy most are the parts most would hate; isolation, idleness, a never-ending sea breeze, an honest day's painting, oiling, then painting some more."

"The occupation strikes me as one best suited for a madman, yet you are of sound mind."

"Going mad is a lighthouse-keeping hazard. Being a sea-faring man, you must know of madness all too well. I understand it inflicts sailors with regularity on the open sea."

"Are you calling me mad?" Rip smiled a dazzling

display of pearly whites through his beard. His teeth were no longer the crooked, rotted stubs they were in the castle.

"What do you call someone who sleeps years upon years of his life away?" Deacon ventured.

"Lucky," Rip responded without hesitation.

"How so?"

"What finer style of consciousness is there? Would you rather be awake, dragging yourself through each dreadful day with the leaden burden of responsibility, and the endless ailments of age? Would you rather be *dead*? Every moment of the dream is a bold, beautifying adventure."

"Some would say the waking world is a far more genuine adventure," Deacon suggested, overly careful with his choice of words. "What is more perilous than the constraints of mortality, the cadence of time, the lack of control?"

"Why do you think we dream?" Rip asked.

Deacon had no answer to the seemingly obvious question.

"We dream to escape the cruel confines of Wakefulness, if only for a little while. We close our eyes each night before bed, and we wish. We wish where we would most like to be, who we would most like to be. In sleep we are transported there, transformed to them. Most who escape in the night accept they will be recaptured by the morning. I have outmaneuvered morning."

The two finished their dinner in silence. They were served a sweet apple tansey with cold cream for dessert. Sweeter than the dessert was the ruby port wine served afterward. Deacon drank his fill of the sweet spirit, and then some. With the help of the wine, the faun found the courage to ask all those questions he dare.

"Tell me captain, how is it you sleep so deeply?"

"I cannot wake. I am a dream."

"That you are not," Deacon corrected. "You sir, are an obstinate dreamer."

"I was that. Now, I am like you. I am an idea."

"An idea of what? Chaos, madness, tragedy?"

Rip downed his glass and rose from the table. He paced the deck awhile, looking up to the misty moon for some answer. A cool breeze penetrated the damp air, gently shaking the ship lanterns, which cast rollicking shadows on the sea.

"I am an idea of insurrection. What began as my own insurrection from the domestication of Dame Van Winkle has swelled to far more. I am a symbol of rebellion against all those dreams of old, and all of their antiquated insanity. I am the vanquisher of all those charlatan-kings, false idols, unjust social contracts, unfair societal expectations, of the past itself..."

"The vanquisher of Faerie," Deacon added, with more than a hint of resentment.

"I have vanquished hundreds of such kingdoms."

"Why?"

"It is the will of the world. Over all this time, I have amassed slumbering legions of peasants, peons, slaves, and serfs. The dreamers of this age demand a new mythos, one without divine right and subjugation. The commoner has come to realize he himself is divine. Vassals have wakened to the fact they are equal to kings, rather than equally inferior."

"Vassals have wakened, but you have not. What will you do? Dream until the end of time?"

"As you well know, time is of no consequence here. We do not track it, though we often traverse it. Here on the Sea of Dreams, Tomorrow and Yesterday are merely destinations."

Long John Silver hobbled up with a fresh carafe of wine. Rip thanked him, and returned to the table. Deacon drank more, and the more he drank the more freely he spoke.

"Though time be a destination, you remain bound by it," Deacon explained. "Time pursues you, even here. One of these days it will find and wake you, as it does everyone."

"Time will lose itself in pursuit of this vessel. Did you know our own boatswain is a ticking, tocking grandfather clock? Old as the hills. Poor chap suffers from dementia. He is often lost, because there is nothing so common in this world as lost time. We lose time, then time finds us. Although I have lost time, I have no worry it will find me again. I am on a quest, one that outpaces time."

"A quest for what?"

"For what else, but a princess. As I said, it is a timeless quest. This particular princess is most elusive. She waits for me in every one of these imagined kingdoms I conquer, yet I can never quite reach her. The moment I arrive, she disappears. Did you not see her waiting for me on the castle walls?"

Deacon, alarmed at the all-knowing question, gave no answer. He remembered the dreaming apparition on the castle walls all too well. It was the grown-up little girl he had discovered with the boy Rip all those years ago, playing at forfeits in the field of flowers — Rosie.

"Do you know why you were captured, and not killed?" Rip asked.

Deacon switched from wine to water, taking a suddenly sober sip.

"We captured you because you are the lighthouse

keeper. You are the one who illuminates the furthest reaches of this eternal fantasy. You are the one who navigates the fantasizer, who grants sight to the stargazer. You are the last light in the night. You can show me the way."

"Show you the way to where?"

"To her, of course."

Deacon, finally realizing his purpose on board the ship, let his thoughts be known.

"She is gone. Time may not have caught you, but it has passed you by. You remain here, yet she has not."

"Where has she gone?" Rip asked.

"She has gone to where the winds of time carry everyone — Tomorrow."

"Then you will show me the way to Tomorrow, without the winds of time to carry us."

I dreamed, one night, that I was having an argument with one of the waiters as to what was the correct time. I asserted that it was half-past four in the afternoon: he maintained that it was half-past four in the middle of the night.

With the apparent illogicality peculiar to all dreams, I concluded that my watch must have stopped; and, on extracting that instrument from my waistcoat pocket, I saw, looking down on it, that this was precisely the case. It had stopped — with the hands at half-past four. With that I awoke.

I lit a match to see whether the watch had really stopped. To my surprise it was not, as it usually is, by my bedside. I got out of bed, hunted round, and found it lying on the chest of drawers. Sure enough, it had stopped, and the hands stood at half-past four.

The solution seemed perfectly obvious. The watch must have stopped during the previous afternoon. I must have noticed this, forgotten it, and remembered it in my dream. Satisfied on that point, I rewound the instrument, but, not knowing the real time, I left the hands as they were.

On coming downstairs next morning, I made straight for the nearest clock, with the object of setting the watch right. For if, as I supposed, it had stopped during the previous afternoon, and had merely been rewound at some unknown hour of the night, it was likely to be out by several hours.

To my absolute amazement I found that the hands had only lost some two or three minutes — about the amount of time which had elapsed between my waking from the dream and rewinding the watch.

This meant, of course, that the watch had stopped at the actual moment of the dream. The latter was probably brought about by my missing the accustomed ticking. But — how did I come to see, in that dream, that the hands stood, as they actually did, at half-past four?

If anyone else had told me such a tale I should probably have replied that he had dreamed the whole episode, from beginning to end, including the getting up and re-winding. But that was an answer I could not give to myself. I knew that I had been awake when I had risen and looked at the watch lying on the chest of drawers.

Yet, what was the alternative? "Clairvoyance" — seeing across space through darkness and closed eyelids?

~ *A dream of philosopher J.W. Dunne,* 1898

Tomorrow is a Wedding Feast

DEACON AGREED TO HELP GUIDE RIP AND HIS CREW TO Tomorrow in exchange for his own safe passage back to the present. Rip made it clear that Deacon's safe return home was subject to their discovery of Tomorrow. Should they not reach Tomorrow, Deacon would not reach home. The faun's fate was far from clear in that scenario.

Deacon was not certain of the exact route to Tomorrow. He knew the general direction, but not the passage. The Sea of Dreams consisted of innumerable bank-less rivers, each with its own unique current. Some ways led to the morning, others to the moon. Many led to nowhere. Some led to somewhere. More went on forever and ever.

The voyage to Tomorrow would be an exhaustive one. Deacon instructed Rip to have the entire crew row with all the force they could muster against the winds of time, in search of those surface waters pulled not by the present, but by possibility. Rip did as the faun advised. The ship started toward what they hoped was Tomorrow, followed by a fleet of roving dreamers.

Deacon's dungeon was upgraded to a luxurious private cabin, complete with bed and bath. There was an extra-large porthole with a view of the sea just above the waterline. On the opposite wall was a watercolor of the same porthole and sea, creating a fanciful mirror-like effect in the room. The space looked more suited for a captain than his captive.

Deacon sought out routines and quickly found one aboard the ship. His mornings were spent on deck playing the navigator, recommending this or that change in course, hoping with each passing day there would be some sign of progress, though there rarely was. He passed the afternoons in his cabin doing those things a lighthouse keeper does: writing, whittling, or just watching and waiting. Mostly waiting. He waited for Tomorrow, but it never came.

Deacon encountered Rip only on those darkest of nights, when the sea would mirror the stars so perfectly, the horizon line on the water would disappear. The two would dine together on deck, in the center of their own pitching and rolling galaxy. Deacon would tell Rip stories of lighthouse life, of beacons and breakwaters. Rip would tell Deacon stories of the world underneath it, of serpents and Scylla. The two became fast friends.

THE CREW ROWED TIREDLY ON INTO THE UNKNOWN. The fleet of dreamers attempted to follow, but gradually faded away, the winds of Wakefulness possessing their sails and crews. It wasn't long before Rip's ship was all alone at sea, with no sign of any port of call, let alone their destination. The days and nights passed, always without a

Tomorrow. Deacon had become drearily anxious at the prospect of their being hopelessly lost when they were found.

Deacon woke in his cabin one morning to an unexpected sight through the porthole. The sea had changed color from its usual deep blue to a clearer turquoise. The boat floated lower in the water, so that Deacon could see above and below. Above was typical. Below was not.

The water was filled with dreams, and not of the sort one has in the middle of night. These were wakeful dreams; hopes, desires, and expectations. There were wishes everywhere. It was as though a bottomless wishing well had erupted to fill the sea. Deacon watched with wonder as the ship sailed through every single wish ever wished. There were children's wishes: toys of every design imaginable flitted by, everything from jack-in-the-boxes to jigsaw puzzles. There were children. They all had wings, soaring here and there, because every child wishes they could fly. Waterproof bonfires shone from the seafloor below, complete with music and dancing. Deacon could hear their distant chorus of wishes. Silver and gold coins swirled about like shining clumps of seaweed. The wishes were a sure sign they were near Tomorrow, because that is where wishes reside.

Deacon rushed to the top deck. He found most of the crew already there, peering over the sides of the ship into the strange seas. The ship itself drifted speedily along toward a gathering gray in the distance. Rip stood at the wheel.

"We have been sailing toward that storm for some time, yet we appear to come no closer," Rip observed. "What do you make of it, lighthouse keeper?"

"It is a sure sign we are near to your destination, captain. Have you not seen the wishes in the water? The storm is further evidence of our arrival. Those gray clouds are the shadows of things to come, of misadventure, tragedy, of death. Here, they must remain at a distance."

"Keep a course toward those storm clouds!" Rip commanded as he looked toward them through his spyglass. In the ashen sky he saw faces faded with age, hearts swollen with grief, and promises burst to raindrops. The furthest skyline was filled with more ruinous expectations.

The ship sailed on, the storm always in the distance. They left no wake because there was no longer a past. Tomorrow was all around. The first sight of it on land was the Ferris wheel carriages bobbing up and down over the horizon as they spun round. Sailing closer, the crew was astonished by the futuristic apparatus. Ferris wheels wouldn't be invented for another one hundred years. That Ferris wheel was hundreds of feet high and filled with riders who laughed and waved at the ship as it sailed by.

They passed more peculiar islands, each its own unique paradise of the hereafter. There was a jubilant harvest festival, where the hooting and hollering of children at play pranced over the sea. A wintry Christmas morning lived on one snow-covered island. Another island was occupied by a single cottage, where the cries of a newborn baby could be heard. They sailed slowly by a chain of tropical islands. A castaway lived on each one, content in sunny seclusion.

One especially colorful island was draped in an immense circus tent. The ship passed close by, giving the crew a good look inside. Under the tent was everything one would expect from a circus, except more so. A colossal, grizzly-bearded woman stood in the center ring, a circle of actual grizzly bears dancing around her. A wider circle of spasmatic clowns paraded around them. Winged monkeys swung wildly from the trapeze. Elephants rode bicycles. More monkeys rode elephants. The dwarfish ringmaster acted as conductor of the absurd opera, occasionally gesturing to the crowd, who laughed so loudly they made waves in the water.

The islands were ideas of the future, of all the hope and happiness we presuppose. They were the mirages used to escape the suffering of today, and to heal the trauma of the past. Rip sailed on, constantly on the lookout for his own idea of Tomorrow. He would not have to look long.

The ship came upon a large, forested island. Its trees were splendidly stained with autumn. Alluring as it was, they would have passed it by were it not for the music coming from it. There was a particular song that evoked a memory for Rip. He knew then that he had arrived.

THEY BEACHED ON A WIDE, GRASSY SHORE. RIP LEFT the ship untethered, as though he did not care to ever sail it again. He slithered down the rigging off the side of the ship with Deacon and the crew hurrying to follow. They ventured across the beach, up and around the meandering dunes toward the woods. The winds rose as they approached the tree line, the forest wailing a welcome.

They discovered a trail that led to the center of the island, in the direction of the music. The song that played for their march was one of those rare masterpieces heard only in dreams. Few remember such songs. Those lucky ones captured in dreams and written upon waking are well known. Paul McCartney dreamt the melody to "Yesterday." Fast asleep one night, Jimi Hendrix strode through a

"Purple Haze" in the Sea of Dreams, which would inspire the anthem. Rolling Stones, R.E.M., Buddy Guy and countless other artists have recorded such dream music.

Marching in single file, between the sounds of their own voices and the blowing forest, the music grew louder, and they knew they were near. The trail climbed a steep sand dune at its end. They crawled slowly up and reached the hilly boundary of the woods.

Looking down, they beheld a little village within a little valley, split by a bubbling brook with cottages on either side. The village was bustling. A pavilion tent rose from the center of town. Long tables were set out with food and drink. Children ran wild through the streets. Couples danced here and there to the music. Villagers warmed themselves around a bonfire. There could be only one explanation for the celebratory scene. It was a wedding feast.

Colonial weddings were far different than those of today. Weddings back then were more free and easy than extravagant. There were no white dresses, multi-layered cakes, wedding halls, programs, or pictures. Weddings were generally held at the bride's home, or in some public space. The finest of wedding feasts might last several days. Judging from the rapturous condition of the villagers, that particular wedding was at least several days old.

Rip leapt hurriedly down the dune to join in the marital merrymaking. He didn't know who was getting married, nor did he care. He was drawn to the village by a sense of urgency he did not understand and could not control. The crew followed their captain. Deacon trotted behind at a respectable distance, unsure of what they were getting themselves into.

Walking into the village, they encountered cheerful

men guzzling greedily from giant-sized tankards. Women sipped silver champagne from goblets of gold. Maidens stood in a circle with arms linked around some red-faced bachelor, some smiling seductively, others dancing wildly. A scantily clad burlesque dancer pedaled through mid-air on a flying bicycle, the wind hiking up her skirt as she sang with those below. Children were everywhere. Girls chased boys. Boys chased girls. The falling autumn leaves caught them all.

The seamen were welcomed to the wedding feast as if they were long-awaited guests. Several snickering women grabbed hold of Rip and danced bewitchingly around him. They lifted their dresses and tapped bare feet on the grass with a force that shook the whole island. Rip was standing there in surprise when a burly bachelorette swept him off his feet, dramatically dipping him to roars of laughter and applause from the crowd.

A band of pie-eyed men hoisted Deacon upon their shoulders. They carried him like some goat-emperor to a tremendous barrel of lager. They filled an equally tremendous tankard for him, hoisted their own, and sang a song:

WHERE SUNLESS RIVERS WEEP
 Their waves into the deep,
 He sleeps a charmed sleep:
 Awake him not.
 Led by a single star,
 He came from very far
 To seek where shadows are
 His pleasant lot.

. . .

172

HE LEFT THE ROSY MORN,
  He left the fields of corn,
  For twilight cold and lorn
  And water springs.
  Through sleep, as through a veil,
  He sees the sky look pale,
  And hears the nightingale
  That sadly sings.

REST, REST, A PERFECT REST
  Shed over brow and breast;
  His face is toward the west,
  The purple land.
  He cannot see the grain
  Ripening on hill and plain;
  He cannot feel the rain
  Upon his hand.

REST, REST, FOR EVERMORE
  Upon a mossy shore;
  Rest, rest at the heart's core
  Till time shall cease:
  Sleep that no pain shall wake;
  Night that no morn shall break
  Till joy shall overtake
  His perfect peace.[1]

DEACON DRANK HIMSELF STUPID. RIP DANCED HIMSELF
silly. The villagers were flawless in their revelry and

173

everything else. None were of ill health or temper. There were no beggars or braggards. No liars or louts. The food was plentiful and perfect. The drink was dizzying, but not too dizzying. The music was as harmonious as the rest of the wedding feast.

The autumn day was perfect as the party. A ginger wind came laden with the sweet-smelling remnants of summer. The sun sat unmoving in the sky, at that transitory moment of dusk when blue and burgundy surrender to purple and pink. Twilight cooled the guests from the cloudlessness above, the breeze blew them along from the past left behind, and the birds chirped in glee from all around.

There was never a more magnificent wedding feast, because it had yet to happen.

IT IS IMPOSSIBLE TO KNOW THE AMOUNT OF TIME RIP and Deacon stayed at the wedding feast. It may have been months, even years. The two were in no condition to keep track of time. Even if they had wanted to, it would have been impossible. Time is non-existent in such ecstasy.

At some point, Deacon took notice of another faun. The faun stood on a tree stump, playing at his pipes like the god Pan. Next to him was a fiddle-plucking dwarf. Leaves from the trees blew overhead in melodic chorus. The odd trio made music that sounded both merry and mystical, like a siren song for the freeing of the soul rather than its capture.

Even in dreams, a faun is a rare creature to behold. Deacon had met few of his kind, so was eager to make his acquaintance. He filled a glass of sparkling wine for the faun and made his way over. Rip broke away from a mob of admirers to join him.

"Good day," Deacon greeted the faun, who happily took the glass.

"A day without end," the faun greeted back before downing the drink in one spectacular swig. "How strange it is to be thirsty, have a drink of something to quench that thirst, then to be even thirstier than before. I am parched almost to death after one sip!"

"The notes of pine, thyme, and lost time have that effect," Deacon explained. "Your songs have an equally enchanting effect. Tell me, what sort of music do you play? I have not heard anything like it in all my days."

"These are songs of forgetfulness. Why, haven't you already forgotten yourself entirely?"

"I... I suppose I have," Deacon found he could hardly remember anything about himself, or anything else. In fact, he had no idea where he'd come from, or why he was there. He looked down at his drink, wondering how many he'd had.

"Here in Tomorrow, there is no Yesterday," the faun continued. "Without a Yesterday, there is no sorrow or suffering. Tomorrow is all hope and happiness. That is why the village is so blissful. That is why we are at a wedding feast."

"Who is getting married, by the way?" Rip interjected.

It was a good question. There was no easy way to tell. Brides of the era did not wear the easily distinguishable white wedding dresses of today. They simply wore the nicest dress they owned. Grooms were just as indistinguishable.

"I beg your pardon." The faun turned to Rip in surprise. "Didn't you know?"

"Know what?"

"Sir, this is *your* wedding."

---

1. *Dream Land,* Christina Rossetti, 1862

When I placed my head on my pillow, I did not sleep, nor could I be said to think. My imagination, unbidden, possessed and guided me, gifting the successive images that arose in my mind with a vividness far beyond the usual bounds of reverie. I saw — with shut eyes, but acute mental vision, the pale student of unhallowed arts kneeling beside the thing he had put together. I saw the hideous phantasm of a man stretched out, and then, on the working of some powerful engine, show signs of life, and stir with an uneasy, half vital motion. Frightful must it be; for supremely frightful would be the effect of any human endeavor to mock the stupendous mechanism of the Creator of the world. His success would terrify the artist; he would rush away from his odious handywork, horror-stricken. He would hope that, left to itself, the slight spark of life which he had communicated would fade; that this thing, which had received such imperfect animation, would subside into dead matter; and he might sleep in the belief that the silence of the grave would quench forever the transient existence of the hideous corpse which he had looked upon as the cradle of life. He sleeps; but he is awakened; he opens his eyes; behold the horrid thing stands at his bedside, opening his curtains, and looking on him with yellow, watery, but speculative eyes.

~ A dream of Mary Shelley, 1816. The dream inspired her first novel, Frankenstein.

A Beard Tangled in Dreams

RIP SPAT OUT A MOUTHFUL OF CHAMPAGNE SO luminous it looked like a regurgitated ray of sunshine.

"Me... *Married*? Why in heavens... What in the name of... Where, when is the ceremony? And to whom am I betrothed?"

"Look, over there," the piper faun pointed to a hill crowded with guests on the edge of town, where the ceremony looked ready to take place. The dwarf grinned as he began in the playing a slow, processional song on the fiddle. "You are late!"

Rip dropped his glass, straightened his coat, smoothed back his hair, and started toward the hill. What else was he to do? It was his wedding day. Rip may have been a rapscallion, but he was an honorable one. He would not disgrace his bride, whoever she turned out to be.

Deacon followed Rip to his fate, as did the remainder of the village. Even the dwarf and faun paraded along, playing at their instruments like a two-man marching band. It seemed Rip was the only one who hadn't known that it was his wedding. Many of the guests clapped him on the back with words of congratulations as he walked on.

"May you be poor in misfortunes, and rich in horizontal refreshment," winked one.

"To love and laughter, happily ever th-after," slurred another.

"Keep ole' jinglin' johnny in your trousers," cackled an old maid.

When Rip reached the base of the hill the guests moved aside all at once, creating a proper wedding aisle for him. He looked up it and beheld his bride all alone on the hilltop. She wore a simple festival dress. The bodice had a low, square neckline edged with lace, leaving little below it to the imagination. Her bonnet cast a shadow over her face, so he couldn't quite make it out. Her shape was voluptuous and vaguely familiar.

Deacon followed Rip up the hill as if he were the best man, when in reality he was the only man. The rest of the crew had disappeared. When, and where they disappeared to was hard to say. Perhaps they woke up, never again to follow their secretive skipper at sundown. Maybe they weren't dreaming at all. Maybe they were ideas, impressed to service by the imagination.

Rip was joined halfway up the hill by a priest who would administer the wedding rites. When they reached the top, the crowd formed a tight circle around them, staring in expectant silence.

"No turning back now," Rip admitted under his breath. The bride stood in the center of the circle, awaiting her groom. She stood eerily still, her face turned away. Rip might have mistaken her for some finely dressed scarecrow, were it not for her hair flitting in the wind.

Rip went to his bride. He thought to at least introduce

himself before they were wed. She looked away from him, at the always setting sun. Rip gave her a hopeful tap on the shoulder. He hoped she was friendly and beautiful. He hoped the ceremony would be a quick one, so he could return to the festivities. He hoped for a continuance of the wedding feast, for a rejoicing without end.

His bride turned to face him, and his hopes were annihilated. He knew her all too well. Indeed, he was already married to her. It was none other than Dame Van Winkle.

In that moment, time finally found Rip. He aged several years in an instant. His eyes sunk in surprise. His skin wrinkled with dread. His back bent in shame. The change was most noticeable in his beard. It dropped from his neck to his waist like a fallen scarf. Its color changed from coffee to cream. The thick hair turned thin and became tangled in dreams. There were ghosts, goblins, castles, curses, and kings. They slithered about in the bristly hairs like living lore.

Dame Van Winkle did not look the least bit surprised. She looked delighted. She smiled as the onslaught of years consumed her evasive husband. But her features would also soon change. They had to, because time had not only found Rip, it had found her, and everything else. The sun finally set. The seasons changed. The everlasting present gave up the day. Dame Van Winkle gave up the ghost. Rip watched as the skin on her face peeled away, exposing a haggard skeleton. The moon rose, bleaching the bride's bones a deathly white.

Deacon was aghast. He watched as Rip backed slowly away, stumbling over a tangle of roots onto his back. He scrambled up, then tripped again over his own never-ending beard. He lay there looking hopelessly around, pleading speechlessly for help. The crowd had disappeared. The village looked abandoned. Deacon was the only wedding guest left.

Deacon helped Rip up and rushed him down the cursed hill. The wrathful remains of Dame Van Winkle gave chase. The two raced through the deserted village lanes toward the woods, wifely bones rattling behind all the while. Deacon hoped to lose the skeletal spouse in the darkness under the trees. If not there, surely they would escape her aboard the ship, at sea.

Deacon and Rip burst through a hedgerow bordering the forest. They ran as fast as they could, but Dame Van Winkle remained close behind. Rip, newly aged as he was, ran slower than Deacon, but faster than his undead wife. After a long while, they finally lost sight of her. Believing they were safe, the two stopped to catch their breath.

The pair made their way toward shore where they hoped to sail safely away. They decided it best to cut through the dense, pathless forest to avoid Dame Van Winkle. They walked quietly on, well concealed by the dark woods. If not for the scattered pillars of moonlight shining through chinks in the leaves they would have been utterly lost. The trees and undergrowth were thicker and more tangled than they appeared, so they didn't get on very fast, but they found their way.

Emerging from the forest, they saw the beached ship in the distance and what looked like the sea beyond. Relieved, they scrambled across the dunes toward it. Relief turned to disbelief when they found the ship. It looked to have been freshly painted green but wasn't. It was drenched in algae and seaweed. The hull of the ship was rotted and filled with holes. The rudder was suffocated with mussels. The main mast and sails were gone altogether.

Time had passed the ship, along with the rest of the island. It was no longer seaworthy, and even if it were, there was nowhere to sail it. The sea had disappeared. In its place were endless, undulating hills. As Rip and Deacon looked out across the barren expanse, they heard a rustling of leaves from within the forest. Turning, they saw traces of white within the trees.

A single skeleton emerged from the tree line. Then another, and another after that. Soon, there were hundreds. They were all the same size and shape. All stared at Rip with two empty eye sockets. All raged from years of resentment. All Dame Van Winkle.

All at once, the cadaverous army charged maniacally at Rip and Deacon. Rip grabbed a rusty musket from where it dangled on the rigging. He carefully aimed, then fired a single shot toward his attackers. The musket ball crashed into an unlucky skeleton with a glass-shattering sound but did little to slow the assault. Not that Rip had meant for it to slow the assault. He just wanted to shoot his wife while he had the chance.

The skeletons were made all the more furious by the shot. They charged over the sand, running faster than ever toward the ship, howling like an ensemble of banshees. Rip and Deacon ran off into where the sea had been, now endless open fields. The two ran and ran, because running was the only option. There was nothing, and nowhere to hide.

It wasn't long before Deacon and Rip lost one another. Their parting was no accident. Deacon thought it best to simply turn aside. The Dame Van Winkles hardly noticed. They were not in pursuit of him. The faun ran and ran, until he'd run all the way home. He went the inevitable course of all dreams, the one where Tomorrow confuses itself with Yesterday, a safe distance from Oblivion, ever so near to Wakefulness. In that place stood the lighthouse he called home.

Meanwhile, the elderly Rip ran until his body felt on fire, head to toe. The soles of his feet sizzled with every step, as though the fields were a fresh hell burning beneath him. His gangly arms dangled exhaustedly from his side. His back ran out of sweat to cool it. His head was dizzy, begging for relief, begging for him to stop.

Just when it seemed Rip could run no further, he came upon a promising sight. A short distance away were a series of high hills, lined with grapevines. The rows of vines were so perfectly straight, Rip guessed them to be part of a vineyard. He was hopeful he could outmaneuver the pursuing wives within the vines, then perhaps find a winery or somewhere else to hide.

The vineyard proved useful in losing the Dame Van Winkles. Rip zig-zagged his way through the grapevines, losing one wife here, another there. An especially dogged gang of Dame Van Winkles were nearly upon him, when he crossed grapevine rows and found himself out of their line of sight for a few precious seconds. He took full advantage, diving into a dark, grape-filled ditch.

Rip lay there as still as could be, watching the brigade of bones cackle by at a predatory speed. It was many minutes before he dared move a muscle. He lay there, convulsing from the exhaustion and fear, teeth chattering, heart bouncing the beard on his chest. He prayed that his own personal closet of skeletons had been fully emptied and forever lost.

Rip eventually ventured up from the ditch. The night was silent and still, with no sign of a single Dame Van Winkle. He wandered through the grapevines like a ghost himself, all faded and forlorn. He staggered on alone, without direction or resolve.

He discerned a faint, orange glow at the top of a hill, near the end of a long aisle of grapevines. The glow was from a single candle. It lit the winery. Making his way up the hill, the shape of the place came into view. It was a little white farmhouse. Through the dining room window sat a woman. Rip knocked on the front door, unsure of what to say, or what he even wanted.

The door opened the moment after Rip knocked, as if he were expected. The woman who answered it was middle-aged. Her blonde hair was flecked with gray, and her blue eyes had faded to silver. She was far older than when he'd last seen her (as was he), but he recognized her at once. It was Rosie.

"I was just waiting for you, old friend. Do come inside."

Spellbound, Rip did as he was told.

"Sit across from me." She smiled. "Would you like some wine?"

"Yes, please." Rip collapsed into the chair, hastily smoothing out his hair and beard. "How... How did you recognize me? This beard hides the boy I once was."

"I remember you like it was yesterday."

"Only, we are in Tomorrow."

"Is that where we are?" She poured him a glass of red wine.

"Yes. We are in a dream."

"I thought so. You look like a dream."

Rip quickly drained the glass of wine. It was too sweet to be real, as were its effects. After just one glass, all the wounds and weariness from his many slumbering crusades were cured.

"This is the finest wine in all the world," Rip proclaimed.

"It truly is a once-in-a-lifetime vintage. I wonder when these grapes were harvested? It tastes less like the past than the future. If I had to guess, I would say this is a wine made from grapes yet to be grown. Perhaps this dream we find ourselves in transcends time."

"I believe we are where time ends," Rip suggested.

"And where would that be?" Rosie asked as she refilled his glass.

"It is where we were always meant to be. Call it what you will: fortune, fate, destiny..."

"This little winery is your destiny then?"

"You are the destiny. The winery is just somewhere. We may as well be anywhere."

Rip waved his hand, and the small room was suddenly transformed into a majestic dining hall. A roaring fireplace illuminated a high ceiling of sparkling chandeliers and ornate tapestries. Rip gave another wave, and the walls faded away. The two found themselves in the middle of a meadow under a moonlit sky. The scene quickly transformed once again. A roof formed over their head, with the same winery returning all around them.

"Tell me illusionist, will we soon wake up?" asked Rosie.

"You will. I will not."

"That is a shame. I should like to stay with you awhile longer. I should like to wake up and see you, to play with you once more, as we played when we were young."

"As would I."

"I have heard it said true love's first kiss would wake even the deepest of dreamers. Do you know the fairy story of the princess cursed to sleep for centuries, only to be rescued by the kiss of a prince?"

"I know it."

"I would kiss my way through all those layers of beard if it would finally wake you."

Rip leaned over the table and kissed her. I'm sorry to say it wasn't a lusty, magical kiss of the sort that rescues princesses or raises the dead. Rip was no prince. As for Rosie, she may have been a princess, but only in dreams. No, that kiss was not of the fairytale sort. It was a parting kiss, given by Rip to Rosie, who knew in her heart of hearts there is no changing a man.

They separated, each pleased with the kiss, but disappointed in the result. Neither had woken up. There would be no breaking of any spell with a kiss. It occurred to Rip then that he was doomed to sleep forever, and Rosie to never meet him in the waking world again.

They looked outside. The sky was brightening. The long night was nearly over.

"Would you like to walk me home?" Rosie asked. "To the dawn, I mean?"

"I should like that very much."

The two left the winery, walking hand in hand through the vineyard toward the first light of the morning. They stopped at the summit of a small hill, where they lay down and waited. Rip closed his eyes as he lay there. Rosie lay with him, using his beard for a pillow. She looked up to the sky, watching all the color of a new day emerge. It wouldn't be long before that new day whisked her away. Before it did, Rip fell asleep.

It was the first time Rip had fallen asleep in twenty years. To fall asleep in a dream is to return to that frequented, oblivious state of consciousness reached only in the deepest of the night. There, the inescapable tides of dreamfulness carry us where they may. Sometimes they carry us through mystical seas, into enchanted forests, with witches and wizards, castles and chaos. Some of those nightly escapades are pleasant. Others are nightmares. Rip Van Winkle's was all of them.

Like all dreams, his would come to end. It would end as it began, with an unspectacular nodding off to sleep in the middle of nowhere. This time he lay with destiny, instead of a dog.

Part Three

Waking Up

A Rude Awakening

Rip opened an eye. Not his mind's eye, but an actual eye. Then he opened the other.

It was the first time in years he'd seen with those eyes, so it may come as no surprise to learn they hardly worked at all. The simple act of opening them was straining. His eyelids were heavy and stuck, like rusty door hinges. When he did finally get them open, it took several minutes for them to adjust to his surroundings.

The first thing he saw were the bones of what he guessed to be a coyote or raccoon. In actuality, they were the bones of his faithful dog Wolf, but there was no way for Rip to know that. There is no accounting for time in dreams. Rip had no idea how long he'd been asleep. For all he knew, it was the morning after that long, drunken night at the King George Inn.

The bones recalled for Rip the first memory from his very long dream. He remembered being chased by the skeleton of Dame Van Winkle for what seemed like an eternity. For the moment, he found he could recall little else of the dream. As the unusual day unfolded, Rip would find himself reminded again and again of events from that longest night.

In those first incredulous moments of morning, Rip wondered if he was experiencing a false awakening. Might it be possible he was still dreaming? No. He couldn't be dreaming, because he couldn't move. Years of repose had withered his muscles away. How those years had not withered him away entirely, this author can only speculate. Perhaps there is nourishment beyond our understanding where we dream.

Rip slowly rose and left the decrepit tree hollow where he lay hidden from civilization for so long. Once outside the tree, he turned to look at it. He found it looked different, more rotted and raven than sturdy and sage. He reached out his bony hand to touch the black bark. The moment he lay a finger on it, the whole tree collapsed into a heap of mossy soot.

Rip backed away, feeling lucky the tree hadn't collapsed on him in the night. He looked around at the fine autumn morning, wondering where his dog might be. He gave a long whistle, but there was no response except for the birds chirping a hello to the strange-looking creature.

Rip turned toward home, dreading the imminent fury of his wife. He hadn't hobbled but a few steps when he realized he was hobbling. In fact, he could hardly walk. His knees ached. His hips throbbed. His back was bent like the middle-aged man he now was. Of course, Rip didn't know he was middle-aged, so sought some other explanation. He wondered if he could be that tired from the night before? Rip had experienced many a severe hangover in his day, but this was something else entirely.

A powerful wind whipped his immense beard up and into his face. He stopped in his tracks, thinking himself bewitched, and not for the last time. He was certain he'd gone to sleep without any trace of a beard. He hated beards. They scratched him awfully.

As Rip made his way through the woods, there were more signs hinting at the passing of years. Firstly, there were less woods. Whole sections of the forest had been cut down, and there were cabins here and there in the place of once crowded groves. Rip noticed a handful of new trees that had sprouted up in once treeless places. A line of skinny cypresses split the wildflower meadow in two. The flowers were all gone, suffocated with an infestation of clover.

Rip returned to that fork in the road where the other, more traveled way led from his own home to town. That road had been transformed from dirt and mud to a crisp cobblestone. Rip was pleasantly surprised, and found the way much easier on his feet, which felt delicate and worn. The few folks he passed on his way looked unfamiliar and strangely dressed. Rip undoubtedly looked equally strange and unfamiliar in the eyes of the passersby.

Rip soon reached his farm, or what was left of it. The house was half-covered in layers of ivy, the other half what remained of the original stone, all weathered and crumbled. The chimney had collapsed on itself. The roof was caved in. The sun rose, shining through the shattered front window, where Rip found himself looking for some sign of Dame Van Winkle. He shook with fear, half-expecting her to waltz out the front door, frying pan in hand for to whack over his befuddled head. But she was gone. Everything was gone.

He started across the field toward his neighbor's house for some explanation, but thought the better of it when he noticed it was painted a different color. Rip's confusion ripened to fear. He and his world were different. He looked around, desperate for some sign of familiarity. He took comfort in the peaks and valleys of the Catskill Mountains. They were dotted with golden tree-tops, the silver river slicing through them like a wave-bladed sword, like always.

Rip was tempted to return to the familiarity of the forested mountainside, but finding himself suddenly famished, decided instead to make his way to the heart and soul of the village — the King George Inn. Surely he would encounter a friendly face there. More importantly, he would learn some explanation for the mystifying circumstances of the day.

Rip's initial encounter at the inn was exactly as it was first described in the original version of this story, written some two hundred years ago:

"HE NOW HURRIED FORTH, AND HASTENED TO HIS OLD *resort, the village inn — but it too was gone. A large rickety wooden building stood in its place, with great gaping windows, some of them broken and mended with old hats and petticoats, and over the door was painted, "The Union Hotel, by Jonathan Doolittle." Instead of the great tree that used to shelter the quiet little Dutch inn of yore, there now was reared a tall, naked pole, with something on the top that looked like a red nightcap, and from it was fluttering a flag, on which was a singular assemblage of stars and stripes;—all this was strange and incomprehensible. He recognized on the sign, however, the ruby face of King George, under which he had smoked so many a peaceful pipe; but even this was singularly metamorphosed. The red coat was changed for one of blue and buff, a sword was held in the hand instead of a sceptre, the head was decorated with a cocked hat, and underneath was painted in large characters, "GENERAL WASHINGTON."*

THE SIGHT OF THE STARS AND STRIPES STOPPED RIP IN his tracks. He recognized them from his long dream, though he wasn't sure of their origin, or meaning. Images associated with the flag flashed before his eyes like individual photographs or paintings, each one a hint as to his connection with the symbol. There was a view of a vast, legendary kingdom in smoldering ruins. Mythical walls collapsed. Fabled towers crumbled. The one true king lay slain on the castle ramparts. Dreamers marched through the city streets in conquest. Rip was their captain. He had fought for freedom from the tyranny of Dame Van Winkle. Dreamers fought for freedom from the tyranny of all that once was. The dreaming triumph over tradition had manifested itself in the waking world as the American Revolution. For what was the Revolutionary War but a toppling of old idols, symbols, and stories?

Rip, the unknowing catalyst for one of the single greatest ideological and societal transformations in the history of mankind, stood outside the inn, fingering his beard, trying to understand what in the name of King George had happened, and why the inn was no longer King George's. Ridiculous as he looked, he wouldn't have to stand there long before someone interrupted him.

"Good day to you, grandfather. Are you lost?" asked a man from the Union Hotel, a hint of whiskey on his breath.

"Grandfather!" Rip stepped back, revolted by the title. "I am a man of but twenty-five summers!"

"Pardon me," the man laughed. "You look ancient, I would guess not a day under fifty-five."

Fifty-five may not sound ancient by today's standards, but it was in fact borderline ancient by colonial standards. The life expectancy in 1787 was just thirty-eight years old.

"What is your name, and on which side did you vote?" the man asked in a more serious tone.

"My name is Rip Van Winkle. I am a poor, quiet man, a native of the place, and a loyal subject of the king, God bless him!"

Unfortunately for Rip, several patrons of the Union Hotel overheard his declaration of fealty to the (former) king. Those patrons informed other patrons, some of whom happened to be veterans of the Revolutionary War. Rip was of course unaware of any war at all having been fought. The hotel quickly emptied. A group of angry men circled the stunned Rip.

"Seems we have a Tory on our hand," muttered one.

"A regular Benedict Arnold, no doubt," shouted another.

"Hustle him! Away with him," the crowd hollered.

"MERCY!!!" Rip fell to his knees, hands raised above his head.

Had Rip been a younger man, he would have undoubtedly been dragged off as a traitor then and there. But old and helpless as he was, the crowd settled down. They began their interrogation, asking where he had come from, and what he was seeking. Rip explained he had come from his farm in search of his many friends who used to frequent the inn.

"Who are these friends of yours? Name them?"

"Vance Van Dijk is my dearest friend in all the territory," Rip declared.

There was silence for a moment, until an old woman replied in a shrill voice, "Vance Van Dijk! Why, he is dead and gone these fifteen years! Dysentery, I think it was... or the measles. May have been both... "

"What about Nicholas Vedder, the proprietor of this establishment?" Rip ventured.

"Vedder sold this place and went off to the army in the beginning of the war. Some say he got blown to bits at Bunker Hill. Others say he was drowned in the Delaware crossing with Washington. All that is known with certainty is he never returned."

Rip was dizzy with confusion. War, Washington, Delaware... There was no sense to be made of any of it. He was distraught at the death of his friend, and so many other changes that seemed to have somehow taken place over a span of many years. The passing of so much time was inconceivable. Had he slept for that long? He felt his beard and began to believe it.

Rip wondered if there was some other mutual friend or relation the crowd might know, when it occurred to him that someone might know *him*, or the man he once was.

"Does anyone here know Rip Van Winkle?" he pleaded.

"Rip Van Winkle!" replied one. "Disappeared in the wilderness some twenty years ago. Heard it told his bloodthirsty wife cooked him for supper. Dame Van Winkle. The ole' battle axe died some years ago herself. Another dysentery that one. Not a single mourner at the service."

Rip smiled for the first time since he'd risen from the dead, but not for long. He had yet to prove his identity to the impatient locals. He suggested the names of other friends and family. All were dead or forgotten. He detailed traditions of the village from yesteryear: the bountiful harvest feasts and midsummer fairs. He spoke of spring-

197

time rituals, where children would go "a-maying," venturing out to gather flowers for planting within town.

The crowd listened with interest, yet remained unconvinced. Seasonal rituals of the sort he described were common throughout the colonies. Making things worse, Rip could not name a single declaration from the Declaration of Independence. Worse than that, he had no idea who was president, or what a president even was. It wasn't long before the crowd lost its patience.

They converged on Rip all at once. He was restrained by no less than four strong men, one for each limb.

"Hang him for a spy," one suggested.

"Firing squad more likely," proposed another.

Things would have gone badly for Rip, had a woman not forced her way through the mob.

"STOP," she ordered. The crowd obeyed.

"You know this traitorous tramp?" they asked her.

"Why, of course. Don't you?" she asked them back. "It is Rip Van Winkle."

The crowd let go of Rip as she strode forward. It was Rosie.

"Rip Van Winkle is dead now twenty years," one man objected.

"Presumed dead," corrected Rosie. She turned to Rip, his memory fresh in her mind from a dream. "I remember you like it was yesterday."

She helped him to his feet as the crowd dispersed. There was no further interrogation needed. Rosie was a respected member of the community, and well known by all in the area. She had grown up in the Catskills, leaving them only to marry. She had recently resettled in the area after the death of her husband, who happened to leave her a small fortune.

Rosie returned home for Rip. She always held out hope he was still alive, perhaps abducted by Indians, or simply wandering on his own accord through the frontier wilderness. Rip was a wanderer, after all. She had finally discovered him wandering after her in dreams.

Rosie remembered the dream of Rip, and the scratch of his scraggly beard as she kissed it. Rip remembered her as well. The face of his dearest friend brought the dream, and every other memory of her, rushing back. Not that Rip needed the dream to recognize Rosie. He would have known her had they been separated for another twenty years.

"Come old friend, I have a carriage in waiting this way." Rosie helped Rip up and along.

The curious crowd watched them from the inn, birthing a legend in their speculations. Where could Rip have been all those years?

"Gone drunk for a decades-long lost weekend in a New York City shanty," said one.

"Continental Army deserter," another guessed.

"Hiding from his wife," others supposed.

But those explanations were far too ordinary for such an extraordinary occurrence. There had to be more sensation to the story. More mysticism. After all, the Catskills where Rip had gone missing were said to be supernatural. So, later that night, after the last whiskey was drunk and the fire burned low, it was agreed as historical fact that the ghost of the great Hendrick Hudson and his lost crew did indeed keep a haunted vigil in the mountains one night every year, at the full harvest moon. They watched over the river named for their captain. They played at ninepins in a hollow of the mountain. They drank an enchanted brew. They poisoned the poor Rip Van

Winkle with such a brew, causing him to sleep the years away.

And Washington Irving wrote it all down.

AS FOR RIP AND ROSIE, PARDON THE CLICHÉ, DREAMS do come true. In their case, it took twenty straight years of non-stop dreaming. The couple lived out the rest of their lives in the grand country estate Rosie had built on the Hudson River with her inheritance. The two roamed the labyrinth of forest trails, gathering wildflowers of every color. They gazed up as the moon bathed the mountain, as they had when they were children. And they fell again in love.

Rip rarely ventured back into town. There was no more Dame Van Winkle to hide from, and his old cronies were all dead or disappeared. He would on occasion have himself a libation at the Union Hotel. There, he would humor his fellow patrons with a tall tale from his twenty years gone. He never denied the legends of ghosts in the mountains or their cursed draughts. That would have been no fun. Besides, he often felt like a ghost himself, come back to life.

Rip took up his old habit of fishing. And just like in the olden days, he hardly ever caught anything. He would fall deeply asleep by the riverside, passing many a pleasant afternoon under the rustling shade of a caring willow. He dreamed in those days, but never for very long, or vividly. Like most, he found he could recall very little from dreams later in life. As we age, Oblivion lures us deeper and deeper, to forests and seas without light or memory, until we finally choose to lose ourselves forever.

One day, napping by the riverside, Rip dreamed of a

faun. He couldn't say for certain what had happened in the dream. It was one of those elusive dreams, remembered only in glimpses, forgotten for the most part the moment the dreamer awakens.

"What does it mean to dream of a faun?" Rip asked Rosie when he returned home.

"I dreamed of a faun once. They are like a dream itself: unexplainable, real as this moment, or not at all. Fleeting. I suppose they are perceived differently by everyone," she surmised. "To me, a faun means magic. What does a faun mean to you?"

Rip thought for a moment.

"Mischief. But in the dream, I think it was I who was the mischievous one."

"I have no doubt of that." Rosie smiled.

"In my time asleep all those years, I dreamt of this same creature. I think he was desperately seeking me out for some reason."

"Dreams are subject to interpretation. Allow me to offer my own," Rosie suggested. "Could it be *you* were the faun? Perhaps you were looking for yourself. I have heard it said there are fragments of our waking selves which live independently in the dream state."

"Perhaps," Rip acknowledged. "My beard is quite goatish, after all."

The Lighthouse Logbook

ONE DAY, DEACON WENT FISHING AND CAUGHT himself a secret.

He caught the secret not far from shore. A crimson wind blew from Yesterday that day, which was where the secret originated. It was an ordinary sort of secret — a tragedy of young love lost. The keeper of the secret, on the other hand, was anything but ordinary.

The mermaid hailed Deacon as he rowed to shore with the catch.

"You promised me a secret," she reminded him. "I see you have just caught one."

"Indeed, I have."

"Is the secret worth telling?"

"Indeed, it is."

"Go on, then. Tell it."

Deacon stopped rowing and stood up in the boat for the telling of the secret.

"Long ago, in a country that was then just a colony there was a boy, who fell in love with a girl. She was his one true love. The two grew up, and wanted desperately to get

202

married, but the boy did not have any money. The cruelest of fates would see to it the two would not wed. The boy would live out his life in secret desire and sadness for the girl."

"You have spun this yarn before," the mermaid interrupted. "It is the tale of Rip Van Winkle."

"No! It is the tale of the *teller* of Rip Van Winkle — Washington Irving. It was his poem I ensnared."

Deacon held the poem up as he read it aloud.

WE LOOK FORWARD TO BETTER HOURS;
What better times can I hope?
My sunny days of youth are over.
Oh, the days, the happy days of youth.
When I lay by the brook and dreamt of love and of distant lands,
When all the distance was so lovely.
Oh, the morning, the sunny, sunny morning of love and youth
Oh, the beauty on which my soul has doted!
The happy bowers, the rosy chambers, the evening walks, the morning greetings—the early days of love.

THE POEM WAS AN UNPUBLISHED ONE FROM THE journal of Washington Irving, dated 1823. The poem was likely inspired by the love of Irving's life, Matilda Hoffman. Hoffman died of consumption in 1807, before the engaged couple could marry. Irving never recovered from her death, and never married. After his own death, Irving's heirs opened a small, locked box to which he always kept the key. Inside it they found a miniature portrait, a lock of hair, and a scrap of paper in Irving's handwriting which read: Matilda Hoffman.

"The stories of Irving and Rip bear a striking similarity," the mermaid pointed out.

"Stories such as these are the stuff of dreams, formed from all those tragedies of fate lived in the day, put right in the night. Few stories truly record the entanglement of night and day, for few truly understand it. The 'two sides to every story' are not right and wrong, his or hers, good and bad. It is night and day. And for every diligent writer, there is a dreamful muse."

DAYLIGHT FADED SWIFT AS A DULL MEMORY. DEACON stored his catch of the day in the library, before brewing a tremendous kettle of black tea. It had been a long day, and a longer night awaited. Tea poured, he proceeded up the spiraling lighthouse stairs to his post at the top of the world.

It was a clear night. The sea was still as a mill pond. It would be an uneventful watch. Toward the end of it, Deacon proceeded to a small desk next to the beacon, where he opened up the lighthouse logbook. The logbook was meant for the recording of the weather and all daily lighthouse station activities. Deacon used it more as his own personal journal.

He opened it and began writing.

IT WAS A RATHER UNEXPECTED DAY AT THE LIGHTHOUSE.
Rose early this morning to find the sun had risen in the wrong direction. This afforded a rare opportunity to paint the Oblivion-facing side of the lighthouse, which never does

seem to get adequate light. Painted all the morning away. Lighthouse looks whiter than these pages.

Had a banquet of cockles and mussels for lunch. Cleaned the kitchen oven.

Played a tune on the old gramophone. I prefer the sound of the gramophone to more modern musical engines. Perhaps that is because I am old myself, and listening not for a better sound, but a lost one.

Spent much of the afternoon atop the lighthouse, tidying up the beacon. Sheen needed shining. Gears needed greasing. Fire needed fueling. Repaired hinge to the door of service room. Split a hoof on the catwalk. Stung like the devil.

Went for a fish. Caught a secret from long ago. It is one I will keep to myself and the mermaid. She was owed a secret.

Started watch at dusk. Pleasant night. Passable chill in the air. Brewed a scalding cup of tea, blacker than a dark roast coffee. As I was finishing in the whittling of a sea serpent, bits of rain started to fall, and not the least bit wet.

The rain was a dusting of daffodils.

The shower of flowers reminded me of that fateful day when I set forth on those strange series of adventures to awaken Rip Van Winkle. Centuries have passed since. How this realm of dreams has changed in those years. Every enchanted forest has been subsumed by a concrete (unenchanted) jungle. Wise wizards have wisely left, and with them all the mystery and magic. Swindlers have stolen the seats of sages. The cruel god kings of old have gone, only to have been replaced with equally vile deities adorned in saintly or political disguises.

I wonder where all the dreamers have gone. People sleep (and dream) less now than ever. Time is money, they say. Sleep is for the weak. Early to bed and early to rise makes a man healthy, wealthy, and wise. I disagree.

This very night, the Sea of Dreams is empty as far as the eye can see. Deep dreamers have all but vanished from this rational age. Fantasy is frowned upon. Imagination is ignored. What is a dream these days but a senseless clumping together of the day's events? They say the path through these dream seas is the path of error. They say the unconscious is best left alone.

I wonder what Rip Van Winkle would say to the American dream of today. I expect he would have no interest in a voyage to Yesterday, or Tomorrow. The simple joys of Yesterday have been so long forgotten no one knows the way there. The seas of Tomorrow are poisoned with profits, their horizon gone altogether, buried beneath mountains upon mountains of material possessions; mansions big enough to house whole Dutch villages of yore, automobiles worth hundreds of harvests, and other meaningless trinkets beyond count, all held together with a mortar of money, printed by men possessed with possessions.

I saw Rip on his final nightly voyage of this life, sailing toward those strange seas I once sailed myself in search of him. I lost sight of him as he disappeared into that immense fog bank, where the beautiful blue sea narrows to a river of darkness and death. I wish he were not dead, but dreaming. I wish he would return, and rally those few dreamers left to a new liberty.

The Rip Van Winkle of old would overthrow the monarchy of the modern era in a single night. Wicked kings and queens of commerce and capital would bow trembling before him in their collapsing corporate cathedrals. Rip and his dream-legions would not stand for all the joyless production and consumption, the dehumanization of machines, the deification of the dollar, and everything else which has corrupted that dream he first designed.

That dream was an ideal. It was a freedom to follow some passion, unbound by the constraints of society. The dream of today is a habit-forming snake oil. It is not a freedom, but a dependence disguised as determination. It is the next 'thing,' be that a drink, dollar, or diamond. It is an impossible-to-reach Tomorrow.

The only genuine path to Tomorrow? Here, today. Tonight! I can see it from the top of this lighthouse. There is a tried and tested current, but for who? Is it for you? Who are you that reads a lighthouse keeper's logbook? Whoever you are, know the beacon remains lit. I hope that you, or someone, will use it.

Setting a course to the Sleeping Siren in a moment. I have a mind to tell the story of Rip Van Winkle to anyone who will listen. Will need a tall glass of remembrance to help in the telling. Oftentimes, the deepest of dreams prove the hardest to recollect.

Good night, and pleasant dreams to you.

Author's Note

Thanks for reading. I had originally wanted to write a book on dreams, not Rip Van Winkle. I encountered Rip by chance one night, somewhere in Yesterday. Or was it Oblivion? Wherever it was, I'm lucky to have found him. I remember how surprised I was to learn there hadn't been a single modern retelling of *Rip Van Winkle*. I hope I did the original tale justice, and that Washington Irving would approve.

Carl Jung and his concepts of the collective unconscious, archetypal phenomena, and the psychological complex were most helpful in writing this. My thanks to him. If you liked this book and are interested in learning more of the dream world, read something by Jung. *Man and His Symbols* is my favorite.

If you enjoyed the story, please leave a review online. I'm an independent author, with no marketing or public relations support from a traditional publisher. Online reviews are critically important in helping to connect me with readers like you.

Lastly, if you'd like to receive future notifications of my upcoming titles, subscribe to my mailing list at https://www.absurdistfiction.com/. I often send out advanced reader copies of new books to that mailing list.

Steve Wiley, Author

Steve is a purveyor of the finest in speculative literature from Chicago. Publishers Weekly called his first novel, *The Fairytale Chicago of Francesca Finnegan*, "Intelligent, enchanting, and playful." Wiley's second novel, *The Imagined Homecoming of Icarus Isakov*, recounts the experience of a mystical tavern serving memories instead of drinks. His short fiction has been published everywhere from Crannóg magazine in Galway, Ireland, to Papercuts Magazine in Pakistan. Steve once passionately kissed a bronze seahorse in the middle of Buckingham Fountain. Seriously, he did.

For new title release and other information, visit Steve's author website absurdistfiction.com. You can email Steve at lavenderlinepress@gmail.com.

Work Cited

- Benjamin Rush's dream. Retrieved from: https://founders.archives.gov/documents/ Adams/99-02-02-5450
- Carl Jung's Dream. Retrieved from: https:// carljungdepthpsychologysite.blog/2020/08/ 31/life-needs-deathcarl- jung/#.YmBXDfPMKuo
- Coleridge, Samuel Taylor. *The Rime of the Ancient Mariner, Lyrical Ballads*. London; 1798.
- De Quincey, Thomas. *Confessions of an English Opium-Eater*. London: 1821, London Magazine.
- Dunne, J.W. *An Experiment with Time*. *London*: Faber and Faber, 1898 (*Dream*), 1927 (*Book*).
- Freud, Sigmund. *The Interpretation of Dreams*. Austria: 1899, Franz Deuticke, Leipzig & Vienna.

Work Cited

- Irving, Washington. *Rip Van Winkle*. London: William Heinemann, 1905.
- King Dumuzi's Dream. Retrieved from: https://www.academia.edu/10098522/Dumuzis_dream_Dream_analysis_in_ancient_Mesopotamia
- Kingsford, Anna. *Dreams and Dream-Stories*. 1888.
- Lord Dunsany. *A Dreamer's Tales*. London: George Allen and Sons, 1910.
- Lord Byron. *The Dream*. 1816.
- Mary Shelley's dream. Retrieved from: https://percyandmaryshelley.wordpress.com/2016/10/27/the-origins-of-mary-shelleys-frankenstein/
- Rossetti, Christina. *Goblin Market and Other Poems*. London: Macmillan & Co., 1862.
- Tolkien, J.R.R. *On Fairy Stories*. Oxford: 1947, Oxford University Press.
- Washington Irving Poem. *The Journals of Washington Irving*. Library of Congress, 1823.
- 17th Century Drinking Song. Retrieved from: http://theappendix.net/issues/2013/7/come-hear-this-ditty-seventeenth-century-drinking-songs-and-hearing-the-past

Printed in the USA
CPSIA information can be obtained
at www.ICGtesting.com
CBHW020658230924
14720CB00014B/638

9 781735 304625